# Lust, Love, & Whatever

D1507175

# Lust, Love & Whatever

## Dr. Manny Rich

THE
ST●RY
PLANT

This is a work of fiction. Names, characters, places, and incidents either are the product of the author's imagination or are used fictitiously. Any resemblance to actual events, locales, organizations, or persons living or dead, is entirely coincidental and beyond the intent of either the author or the publisher.

The Story Plant
Studio Digital CT, LLC
P.O. Box 4331
Stamford, CT 06907

Copyright © 2016 by Dr. Manny Rich

Story Plant Print ISBN-13: 978-1-61188-245-2
Fiction Studio Books e-book ISBN-13: 978-1-945839-02-3

Visit our website at www.TheStoryPlant.com

All rights reserved, which includes the right to reproduce this book or portions thereof in any form whatsoever, except as provided by US Copyright Law. For information, address The Story Plant.

First Story Plant Printing: September 2017
Printed in The United States of America
0 9 8 7 6 5 4 3 2 1

I wish to dedicate this book to the following supervising analysts with whom I worked: Isa Brandon, Arlene Wolberg, Ethel Person, Edrita Fried, Manny Schwartz, Ruth Gruenthal, and most to Nettie Attardo, who was my first supervisor and brought me into the world of being a therapist.

— Manny Rich, PhD

# ONE

I sat in my small office just below Canal Street, stunned, reflective and a bit numb, still gripping the receiver. The phone call had ended abruptly when the caller hung up following a series of expletives and a threat on my life. My mind raced and all I could hear were the fingers of my other hand tapping staccato on my new, high-gloss mahogany coffee table.

The first day I opened my own practice in 1968, I purchased a comfortable club chair and an office chair on wheels. This I used to scoot from spot to spot in my small space to best view the expressions of my patients, to read their thoughts. I bought a Persian throw rug on sale at Macy's and a green footstool from Sears for ten dollars.

On one otherwise bare wall hung a sepia photo of Coney Island, featuring a distant beach. I had taken the picture in 1957 with the first extravagant purchase I had ever made for myself: a thirty-five millimeter camera. Neatly hung over my desk was my diploma and credentials, issued by the officials of NY, stating my right to practice as a therapist. Seven small clocks sat on the desk. In the center was a tiny handmade clock my mother had brought from the old country in her handbag. I had bought the others over the years to keep it company.

Dominating the room was the couch—plush, dark-green fabric with matching pillows, designed to be comfortable for two, with the possibility of a third person, providing they were of modest proportions.

It had been five years since I had hung up my own shingle. Even now there were times I couldn't imagine how this had become my life's calling. An only child of immigrants who had found their way out of Germany before the horrors of Hitler's final solution, I seemed always to be running at breakneck speed, not knowing where I was heading. I finished high school in just under three years and then NYU in an equally short time. Graduate school immediately followed at Evander-Child College, where I finished as a precocious twenty-two-year-old with a piece of parchment representing my degree in social work and no idea what to make my life's mission.

On my "bucket list" was a burning desire to lose my virginity, and so my days were filled with "what ifs" about the hundreds of women, both young and older, who crossed my path. But just as I was always running too fast to commit to a single goal, I couldn't settle on one single girl. I was too afraid to stop running.

Restless and lonely, I took the first job offered to me at an underfunded clinic uptown in Harlem. I approached the work as I did everything, with unbridled enthusiasm and professionalism. Yet my downtrodden constituents were largely disinterested in the wisdom I was offering, despite the fact that my guidance might lead them to form healthier nuclear families and break their endless cycle of broken homes. They saw me as "the Jew," someone who could not really be trusted.

So in less than a year, frustrated by my own dormant sex life and a chaotic work environment of unsolvable challenges, I resigned. Somewhat impulsively, I decided to enlist in the Marines. I figured it would give me time to breathe, examine my passions, get a tattoo and meet a bevy of beauties who would remove my uniform and roll around naked with me. At least that box on my bucket list would be checked!

At the recruitment station in the dank, humid Armory, after a lengthy physical and half a dozen tests, I waited with a couple hundred other lost young men to see if Uncle Sam wanted to take me in as family.

A tall, extremely fit captain bellowed my name and I entered his cramped office. Officer Martin was a no-nonsense, rigid man in his late thirties. He wore a buzz cut and had more metal pinned on his chest than you might find at a chop shop.

"*Meyers, Elias.* Is that short for Elijah?" asked Captain Martin with a tone that threatened a bullet to the temple if the answer displeased him.

"No, sir, Elias, just Elias," I answered, trying to lighten the mood. And then followed with another "Just Elias," as if making sure I had answered correctly.

The humorless officer stared at a chart with my test results. He appeared not to move, not even to blink. The silence between us filled my body with tension. Only the music floating in from an unseen radio kept the situation from becoming surreal.

"Somewhere over the rainbow way up high . . ."

I felt an aching need to fill the silence and so I commented, "You know, sir, that some believe this lyric, 'somewhere over the rainbow,' was a special inspiration for the poor souls in the camps during the war who hoped that . . . I mean, it gave them, well, hope."

The captain shot me a scathing look. "You want to be a marine, son, then don't talk to me about song lyrics unless you want to join the homo brigade!"

Despite my trepidation, I forged on, "Well, sir, I only thought it interesting that a song about leaving home is really about getting back home. You saw the movie, right?"

"Everyone saw that movie." He was nearly shouting. "It's the one with the scarecrow who has no brain. You might as well have played him. If the pieces fit . . . right Elias, just Elias?"

Again, dead silence. He kept looking at my test results and I wondered why for so long? What could he possibly be searching for? The entire clipboard held five or six pages. It wasn't *War and Peace* for Christ's sake.

Finally, "What are you doing here, just Elias?" asked Captain Martin, without taking his eyes off my chart.

"Well, sir, I thought I might see the world, give back to the country. Find my bliss. You know, sir, find my—"

The captain looked at me as if I had a third eye. "Find your bliss!?" he nearly shouted. "What the fuck does that mean? Again, this is the Marines, son. Not some la-la village for homos."

"Perhaps you're misunderstanding what I mean by bliss, sir—"

"Shut up, Meyers. Zip it, Elias just Elias."

What a prick! However, I did what the prick ordered and waited some more. Finally, he shoved back from his desk.

"You're going home, Elias, just Elias. You're too smart to be crawling around carrying a backpack bigger than you. And you're a wimp. You'd last as long as a fart in a January wind. Go back to school, use your mind and figure out a way to help this country get back on its feet. Lots of damaged men out there since the war. Maybe you get them back on track. Huh, son? HUH?"

I wasn't wild about the fart reference but in my wildly beating heart I suddenly realized that I really didn't want a tattoo and sooner or later everyone finds a way to get laid.

"Yes, sir." I rose shakily. "Thank you."

"Just in case you can't 'find your bliss' out there in Homoville come back and apply to officer school. Spend the weekend in Oz wishing for a future rather than making one. Till then I'm busy."

"Yes, sir," I repeated and moved toward the door.

"Oh, and Elias Meyers." I braced for another insult. "Try doing some pushups and eat something."

And with that I found myself back on the street. I wasn't going to be a marine. As I stood on the sidewalk and watched the hundreds of purposeful New Yorkers walk by on their way to wherever, I realized the captain wasn't really a prick but a sort of soothsayer. He sensed that I was meant for something better than crawling on the ground in camouflage and toeing the line. He saw that I had talent and wisdom and heart and released me to explore those gifts. The captain was a life-changer, a man I would remember for the rest of my life.

I took a few days off. I wrote out the words to "Over the Rainbow" and found that it was about a lot more than Judy Garland clicking her heels. I also investigated other songs that were important during the war. My curiosity had been awakened. "I'll Be Seeing You," "Sentimental Journey," "Every Time We Say Goodbye" and dozens more all had hidden meanings. This got me thinking about the human heart, about loss and longing and how the mind must lead the way to salvation. Was I actually inspired?

I did some pushups and ate red meat. I even drank beer at the local bar near the university. And bingo! I finally met a girl! Grace, aside from a mouth full of teeth in need of braces, was hot, eager and experienced. I have no idea how I lucked out. We just fit. Grace needed a reliable man who would provide for her, but was so absorbed in his work that her life was her own. A small red flag, but I was too enamored to care. I was too busy fueling the intensity of what was quickly becoming a relationship, creating magic from the minutiae of daily routine.

After days of not getting out of bed, playing with Grace's busty, satin-skinned body to the soundtrack of popular tunes playing in my head, it came to me. I knew what I wanted to do. Knowing the bliss of a heart, mind and body unified for the first time in my life, I would help others seek wholeness.

I decided to return to school one last time and raced through as if chased by demons, receiving a doctorate in integrative human behavior. I followed that with seven more years earning certification in psychoanalysis, the supervision of the psychoanalytic process, and psychoanalytic community work. Then I did my seven years of residency at the state sponsored hospital near NYU. I joined the staff of their outreach clinic, saw hundreds of patients and heard thousands of stories. Within a year, I was the head of the whole operation.

Much of the work was short term; many patients were too ill, too far gone, with little hope for rehabilitation. Many more regressed in their behavior, to achieve some sense of what they conceived as normalcy. They made poor decisions in order to control their inner landscapes. I heard tales of behavior that made eating human flesh seem a more acceptable option.

It didn't help that most were impoverished. I believed in the teaching of Dr. R. Bak, who said that if "one's reality were harsh, one's fantasies would take the same energy." And I disagreed with Freud, who felt that "personal issues came from distortions in the brain and not from economic conditions." W. Stekel, an acolyte of Freud, believed and taught both positions (which would make a sane man crazy).

I read way beyond the required syllabus and made my own daring, outside-the-box decisions. I was not a follower but one to explore for my own answers to what I observed. Though still a neophyte doctor, I knew that everything was open to interpretation. For almost five years, I listened carefully, learned when to ask the key questions, and knew that only in deep reflection might I find answers.

Clients that made me want to shower following a session might arrive from any part of town, on foot or by limo. I came to believe—in fact, it became my mantra—that there was no such thing as deviant or abhorrent behavior. Whatever helped people find contentment in their sexual relationships was acceptable, with the absolute caveat that no one else was harmed, including unseen harm.

And now someone wanted to harm me. I fought to regain control of my nerves. The caller who had just threatened my life both frightened and enraged me. I had heard threats before in my practice, but I had chalked them up to emotional nonsense. So many clients felt rage; my duty was to be the best doctor I could. As I sat in my office, inert, I realized my fingers weren't tapping on the table—my whole hand was shaking beyond control. I carried a licensed gun, but it was pointless owning a gun that I couldn't even grip. For the first time in my career, I feared for my life.

"I am going to kill you, Dr. Meyers," he had said calmly, as if stating a simple fact. "I blame you for my wife's threats to leave me. Thanks to your Doctor Mumbo Jumbo bullshit she is promising to walk out on me." His voice was not raised. There was no rancor. "And when she does I'm coming to your office and I'll beat you with a tire iron, and then I'll sit on your shrink couch and watch you writhe in pain for a while."

I interjected in vain. "Mr. Todd, it's my responsibility as your wife's doctor to help her. Professional ethics prohibit me from discussing what we talk about together, but I assure you her decisions and actions are hers alone."

He wasn't hearing me.

"Shut up!" he shouted, losing control. "What do you know? She's crazy! Isn't that why she has to see a scumbag like you? You pathetic little kike, playing G-d with other people's lives. You shit!"

Abruptly, the calm, measured voice returned.

"So after you've suffered a whole bunch of hurt I'm going to blow your brains out and kill you. Bye bye."

Then the phone went dead.

I willed myself to call the police. All the previous threats against me hadn't seemed real. This was different. I knew it in my professional brain; I knew it in my gut. Frank Todd was going to kill me. It was just a matter of when.

I called the local precinct, explained the situation to Sergeant McCarthy and implored him to send an officer over to discuss my safety. The cops in the neighborhood knew me and liked me, but the sergeant thought I was overreacting. I insisted.

"OK, OK! I'll send someone over. For the moment, relax."

I hung up, not at all relaxed.

The office door buzzed and I nearly jumped out of my skin. It was four o'clock. Rebecca Dyson! She was a three-times-a-week patient who had missed two weeks, so today would be especially taxing. A normal session with her was tantamount to a week in the Gulag. I buzzed her in and tried to clear my mind.

Rebecca breezed in and took her usual spot on the couch. She seemed more than giddy today, a mischievous smile playing on her pouty lips. She wore a short black skirt, high heels and a lilac silk blouse from which her lacey brassiere peeked. Rebecca kicked off her high heels and then, quite unexpectedly, removed her top and her bra and tossed them aside.

She sat across from me, her naked breasts larger than I had ever imagined, her thirty-something body toned to perfection. For the second time in one day, I fought to regain my professional demeanor.

Rebecca expected a response. I had no intention of providing one. "So?" she finally asked.

"So?" I replied.

She stood up, holding her breasts close to my face. "So what do you think? I had a boob job—went to a Double D. I think my clients deserve it. What's your honest opinion, Dr. Meyers? With these new boobies I'm planning to raise my rates. Fair, wouldn't you say?"

Rebecca wanted me to touch her breasts to see if I thought they felt "real." I did so (I never learned that in any school) and assured her they did. However, her greater concern was whether the breasts would make her more valuable to men. Again I assured her they were fine but were only a small part of her value. Apparently satisfied, she stepped back and picked up her bra just as someone buzzed the door.

"Police, Dr. Meyers. Let me in!"

# TWO

While Rebecca massaged her new Double D breasts back into their cups, the buzz became a pounding.

"On my way, Officer! I'm in session with a patient." I tried not to betray any angst as I unlocked the door.

Rebecca was just beginning to button her blouse as the policeman entered, clearly slowing down for his benefit. He watched as she finished, his gaze lingering on her as she sat down and crossed her long, shapely legs, dangling a pump precariously from her toes.

She was slightly peeved at the interruption and rightly so. I cursed myself for not telling the cop to come back. Another ten minutes and I would have begun to interpret Rebecca's feelings, begun to discover why the size of her breasts seemed to represent her entire worth as a human being. But I had been flustered. Even while she was flaunting them, I could still hear Frank's voice in my head.

"Um, could you excuse us for a moment, Rebecca?"

"Of course, Dr. Meyers," Rebecca purred. "I'll just go powder my nose so you men can . . . take care of business." She stood and smoothed her skirt, never taking her eyes off the cop. And as she passed him on her way out, she "accidentally" rubbed against him like a pussycat against a scratching post.

Officer Stone hid his arousal well, or was simply so well trained that he chose to ignore Rebecca's behavior. Her perfume hung between us in the air.

"Sit down, Officer. Please."

"Thanks, Doctor. And, um . . . Well, I see Ms. Dyson is in rare form today."

"You know her name?" I was somewhat surprised.

"You bet. We all do. She 'owns' the captain to whom I report—bought him with sexual favors, both her own and those of the young girls from that stable she controls. It's an assault on my integrity, but in New York there's unfortunately an unspoken law, 'The Blue Shield.' And I won't be the snitch who ruins my own career for a woman who spreads like butter on warm toast." Interesting imagery from a gumshoe, I thought.

Suddenly Stone went to the office door and opened it quickly as though he expected Rebecca to be eavesdropping on the other side. Then, apparently satisfied she was still off somewhere powdering, he returned and sat across from me.

"Dr. Meyers," he began.

"Elias. Call me Elias. Just Elias is fine."

"Dr. Meyers," the officer began again, "I was asked by my sergeant to look into the threats made against you by a Mr. Frank Todd. After some investigating, I must inform you that this is not someone you should take lightly. We now think he might actually try to kill you."

"I believe it too," I said calmly, but his corroboration made my blood pressure jump. "That's why I called the precinct."

"Your instincts are on the nose, Doc. Todd has a record. In fact, he spent two years in the pen for battery and has a list of domestic violence episodes as long as your arm."

"I'm aware of those issues," I replied. "His wife is my patient and her situation is the catalyst for these threats. She's afraid of him and wants to leave him. Clearly, he blames me—the loss is something he can't handle." I took a deep breath. "What do you suggest I do, Officer?"

"You should file a complaint for harassment and request a restraining order."

"That's a quick way to get dead. We both know that. A restraining order is meaningless. I need an officer assigned to protect me!"

"Dr. Meyers, if it gives you some sense of security, I'll stand guard outside your office door until you've concluded your appointments for the day. At that time I'll escort you to the precinct where we can explore all options, including a restraining order against your nemesis."

I thought "nemesis" was an odd choice of words but accepted his offer to guard me, however temporarily. Again he snatched open the door to catch Rebecca. Coast clear, he stepped into the hall and shut the door.

Minutes passed as I stared at the picture of Coney Island over my couch. Would life ever seem that simple again? As simple as a new camera, a beautiful day and a sea breeze that made me feel that anything was possible? A sharp tap at the door jolted me back. I reached for the .45 Kimber in the shoulder holster I'd put on after Frank Todd's call. Wait. The cop was in the hall. No reason for alarm.

Rebecca's curly blonde head popped around the corner. "I see you have a sentinel in the hallway. Is it safe to come in?"

"Of course, Rebecca. I apologize for the—"

"That's OK. I was waiting for someone anyway— someone who's going to help me with my future. Sort of a sponsor. Hope you don't mind."

"Not at all, Rebecca, let's meet him." I began to rise as she flung the door open; then I froze in disbelief.

# THREE

A Hassid dressed in full regalia—expensive black coat, fur hat, and endless beard—filled the doorframe, towering over the indignant Officer Stone who just managed to squeeze past him, sputtering, "Wait just a minute, bud, you can't just barge in like this!"

The Jew laughed and the massive curls around his ears danced. Deftly, he reached around Stone and extended his hand. "No need to arrest me, Officer! Rebecca invites me, Dr. Meyers."

Surprisingly, the Jewish Paul Bunyan had a dead-fish handshake. I pumped it the best I could.

"Ah, nice to meet you Mr . . . ?"

"Schwartzberg. Moshe Schwartzberg."

"Well, nice to meet you, Mr. Schwartzberg."

"Call me Danny."

"OK, Danny. Please sit down so I can resume Rebecca's session."

Stone stood close by, vigilant as a bulldog.

"Thanks, Officer Stone, I'll take it from here."

With a glare, he went back to his post in the hall.

Danny took a seat next to Rebecca, who had curled up in her usual spot, and kissed her hand gently. "My darling, my sweet *tatala*, you look lovely as always." Then he reached deep into his pocket and pulled out a gigantic wad of one-hundred-dollar bills held together by a gold money clip and threw it on the coffee table. There it sat, reflected on the glass, larger than a grapefruit, probably northward of twenty thousand dollars.

I had learned quickly in my practice that when things don't seem to make sense the best thing to do is remain silent, listen and then speak. I now practiced my own Golden Rule.

"Cash, Dr. Meyers! On your table here I have placed some cash," he said, putting his arm around Rebecca who snuggled up to him, enveloped by his enormous girth.

"You see, Dr. Meyers, Danny paid for my breast enhancement. He and I have been seeing each other for several months now and he's asked that I continue my work for no more than six months and then become exclusive to him."

"You've been seeing this man for several months and never thought to mention it in our work?" I fought to sound objective, but she was pissing me off. "I can't help you if you don't share all truths with me."

Rebecca plowed on, "Danny will back me in my pursuit to leave the escort world and allow me to pursue some of the options that *you* have helped me believe are possible to make a better life for myself."

Danny leaned forward intently. "I want a cash discount on Rebecca's appointments because with that discount I will help finance Rebecca's change of profession. So what do you say? How much discount for my cash?" He spoke with a thick accent, peppered with Vs for Ws, and I struggled not to view him as a caricature.

"The short answer, Mr. Schwartzberg . . ."

"Please call me Danny."

"You know why they call him Danny, Dr. Meyers?" Rebecca blurted out. "Because he's a wonderful singer and everyone loves to hear him sing 'Danny Boy' and so it just sort of stuck as a nickname! Sing it for the doctor, Danny!" She fairly bounced up and down like a cheerleader.

"Oh Danny boy, the pipes the pipes are calling . . ."

Indeed it was an amazing voice, but the situation was far too bizarre.

I stood. "Mr. Schwartzberg—"

"No, no! Danny, please. I want to assimilate into New York world. Be part of the crowd. I have my girlfriend and money and want American future. So please—Danny. OK?"

*Assimilate?* I asked myself. With an accent thicker than sludge in the East River, a backwoods beard, a mortician's black coat and a fur hat, assimilate? And, wearing this Halloween costume, he wanted to prepay for discount therapy and the exclusive services of a high-end prostitute, but only after she continued to work for six months at higher rates because her breasts were bigger? Only in America!

"So you have money and your girlfriend but I see you also wear a wedding ring."

"Of course! I have good Jewish wife and beautiful children. Now I help this sweet girl."

Although this promised to be an interesting continuation of Rebecca's saga—professionally riveting, as a matter of fact—my next appointment would arrive in minutes. My nerves were shot and I had no interest in his "cash."

"Please remove that wad of green and put it back in your coat, sir. I suggest we all meet at Rebecca's next session and further explore the situation."

"But it is cash, tax free monies. Please reconsider this offer . . ."

"It's monopoly money, and I don't play board games," I said, leaving no room for discussion. "My fee is my fee, Mr. Schwartzberg."

"What happened to Danny?" Danny asked.

"He'll be welcomed back when the cash goes away. I'm sorry, but Rebecca's time is up."

Danny looked like a hurt puppy. Rebecca picked up the thousands from the table and quickly stuffed them in her purse and brassiere. She took Danny's hand, pulled him up from the couch and headed for the door.

"See you, Dr. Meyers. Now say goodbye, Danny."

"Goodbye, Danny," Danny said, confused by such a rapid dismissal.

Between her new implants and a bra filled with hundreds of Benjamin Franklins, Rebecca left with a bosom fit for the *Guinness Book of Records*.

As they passed Officer Stone, I heard him say, "But sveetheart it is kash money!" And then they were gone.

# FOUR

Jimmy Sloan was my next appointment.

I needed a few moments to gather myself and get ready for his overwhelming sadness. Although he was making progress, the process was so arduous and the circumstances so disturbing I needed all my fortitude to get through his sessions. I popped two aspirin and chased them with a swig of cognac from the flask in my drawer.

Although he was twenty-three years old, one might guess that Jimmy was sixteen or younger. His body was frail and stooped as if carrying terrible burdens. He wore thick glasses that had been the source of ridicule and bullying for as long as he could recall. Without the glasses he was legally blind. The irony was that Jimmy was a talented painter, and the delicate watercolors he created were clearly an escape from his grotesque situation.

I had met Sloan after the sudden death of his father, the loss of who threw him into a desperate depression. His anxiety was so acute I found myself checking in with him multiple times a day at the outset. Sloan's father had been the boy's rock. Without him, he was dazed and uncertain. With his mother in shock, our sessions were his only hope of moving forward.

As I worked with the grieving boy a disturbing fact emerged. He felt a duty to comfort his mother so he began to sleep in her bed so she wouldn't be alone. Perhaps the initial intent was noble but there were unintended consequences.

They were both so bereft that the relationship moved quickly from sharing a bed to holding his mother in his arms, caressing her in the hope of washing away her grief. The power of their mutual sadness erased the boundaries of her adulthood. Like two lost teenagers, they began to sleep nude in each other's arms. Inevitably, they began to have intercourse every night. She cried out in the confused tumble of her orgasm, "You are saving me! What would I do without you, Jimmy!"

As her sadness subsided, her lust increased.

In contrast, I witnessed the "shrinking" of a young man who was already slight, and the disappearance of his persona as if he were being erased from a sketch—eyes vacant behind his thick lenses. His voice dropped to a slow whisper. It was almost as if he were ceasing to be.

The greatest horror was the deterioration of Jimmy's eyesight due to the emotional carnage. I had taken him to an ophthalmologist who had confirmed my belief: the progressive blindness was brought on by guilt, stress and shame. What a tale of woe! He would sob through every session and plead for guidance, clearly knowing what he was doing was sick; but he was helpless in his mother's grip.

Finally, I insisted that I meet this woman who was having intercourse with her son. His only hope was for me to treat them both. Today's session was the first that Mrs. Sloan would attend. I braced myself and looked at the clock. This brutal day was only half over. I desperately needed to eat but had no appetite. Glancing out the window, I noticed that Officer Stone had taken up a position next to his patrol car and was gazing intently down the street. Had he received some new information?

The Sloans arrived a few minutes late. Jimmy was now wearing dark glasses and carrying a red-tipped metal cane. He tapped his way to the couch and sat. Phyllis

Sloan lingered in the doorway, silent. I nodded and waited patiently. Reluctantly, she sat . . . closer to her son than appropriate. Then she took his hand, held it tightly, rested it in her lap and looked at me defiantly.

She was a handsome woman a few years shy of fifty, her aura that of a rigid schoolmarm, devoid of warmth. Nevertheless, she exuded carnal energy. Tall and lean, she wore dark slacks and a matching blazer over a white silk blouse that revealed modest cleavage. Her auburn hair was pulled back in a demure bun and she wore tiny pearl studs in her ears. In juxtaposition, her long nails were painted blood red like the underbelly of a black widow. (The fantasy was mine casting a negative aura.)

Awkwardness filled the room like thick smoke.

"Jimmy, it's good to see you. How have things been for you this past week?"

"Same, more or less," Jimmy whispered in response.

"Mrs. Sloan, I've thought for quite some time that this meeting is essential to help Jimmy get past his issues, so thank you for coming. In fact, you both have challenges to overcome. And neither of you can heal without the other."

She grew rigid. "Are you suggesting I have caused my son damage by not coming sooner?" She wasn't really seeking an answer.

"I was saying that—"

"I love my son! He has been a gift from G-d in helping me cope with the loss of my husband. I carry the wish for his well-being next to my heart every day, all day. Do you understand that, Doctor?"

"No, Mrs. Sloan, I don't. The behavior you both engage in at home is filling him with so much guilt that his life is one of constant sorrow. Self-esteem is not in his vocabulary. Nor does it help you make a new life for yourself."

"What has he has told you, Doctor?" Her voice was

suddenly high pitched and filled with anxiety. Jimmy sat frozen, his eyes hidden by the dark glasses. "What did you tell him, Jimmy?"

The young man cringed and curled inward.

She turned on me. "Whatever he said is the invention of a troubled boy grieving the loss of his father."

"I don't believe that, Mrs. Sloan, and I'm quite certain you don't either."

"You can't be certain of anything about me, Doctor!"

"I understand you have suffered a terrible loss and have yet to properly grieve."

Her disdain escalated. "It's presumptuous of you to make any commentary about me. We've just met."

"Jimmy is suffering because of the actions you've encouraged him to perform." I measured the words carefully.

"Perhaps my son is suffering due to your poor judgment and the imposition of your will upon him!" She was perspiring now. Wisps of hair stuck to her forehead.

I took a deep breath. "You're having intercourse with your son, Mrs. Sloan—every night for months now. Having sex with your son is confusing, disorienting and it is destroying you both."

Jimmy's cane began a percussive, angry, random beat against the wooden floor.

"How dare you! Jimmy, we're leaving!"

"Healing must be just that, not a situation that creates more sorrow."

"I'm his mother. I love him. Jimmy . . ." She was pulling Jimmy up; I needed to work quickly.

"I know you love him. I know how much pain you've suffered since the death of your husband. But Jimmy is at terrible risk here. He has practically disappeared. If this doesn't end immediately, he has no future. You both need to rejoin a sane world."

She looked surprised. "Sane world? Who are you to

judge—"

"Your love is misguided. You must free your son and I will help. He must—and you must—find friends and a life away from one another. I'll help you seek your own therapy."

"Therapy?!" she shrieked. "You mean with a quack like you?"

"A female therapist who—"

"Male, female, what difference does it make? Another Jew who will drive me further into despair, for a price!"

Jimmy was now banging his cane loudly against the floor and rocking back and forth as if possessed.

I had to raise my voice. "If you continue on this path you'll kill him. I want to help him and I want to get help for you."

"He loves me and we are the only world we need. You can't help us! You can leave us alone!"

Jimmy exploded. "Shut up! Shut up, Mother! You force me to fuck you every night. I can't look at myself or find words to describe my misery." Jimmy's anguish flooded out of him. His mother was horrified. She could not stop his raging words. She started to sob, then rock fro and back. "WHO IS MY SALVATION? Don't you understand? You're supposed to be my *mother*."

The young man stood up and, despite his diminutive size, appeared to tower over her. As he shouted he gathered momentum, courage and purpose. He shook, and it took all his strength to hold back tears and not lose his way.

"Who is there for me, Mother? Answer me. Dr. Meyers says you must let me go, and you won't. Is this the way you show your love?"

I entered the fray, shouting to be heard. "Jimmy, you need to take responsibility for your part in this."

He took in many breaths, gulping for air. In more measured tones he continued. Without the shouting his words were even more powerful. "I must leave you, Mother. I don't believe you meant to hurt me. I obeyed you because you are my mother."

Mrs. Sloan stood up.

I interjected. "Jimmy, name your fear. Tell her why you continued to engage when it made you so miserable."

His voice broke. "I was afraid I would lose you too, Mother."

Mrs. Sloan remained motionless, transfixed, as though seeing her son for the first time.

"Dr. Meyers is right, Mother. I played my part even though I knew and *you* knew how terribly wrong it all was. Today I've lost some of my fear. Not my love of you but my fear of you."

He faltered momentarily, taking another desperate gulp of air.

"I want you to live. I want to live! But allow us to be healthy and separate. I have dreams, hopes, and desires. I'm a man, not your . . ."

He struggled to find a word to bring this to some kind of closure.

She drew back. "Your what?"

"What would Daddy say to me if he knew?" Jimmy asked plaintively.

"Not your what?" she repeated.

Her son stood tall, threw down the cane and removed his dark glasses. He moved closer to her and squinted as if looking at a blazing sun. His eyes found hers and held her stare as tears rolled down the woman's cheeks.

"Lover! I can't be your lover."

A sob escaped her.

"That's not what you want for me, is it?"

Phyllis Sloan reached out wordlessly to touch her son.

Quietly and without rancor Jimmy said, "Please don't touch me, Mother. Those days are over."

No one spoke. I had pushed Jimmy. Yet I had stepped back to let him step forward on his own.

"I can't let you go so fast," she cried.

"I'll make arrangements to stay elsewhere tonight and sometime tomorrow, when you're not home, I'll come by and pick up my things. In time I'll see you and we can meet in a public place. I don't want to lose you, Mother. I simply want to lose what we've become."

Mrs. Sloan took a step back and looked at her son as if she didn't know him which, in fact, was true. Jimmy had turned the page on sorrow and had begun to author the next chapter in his life. After a long moment, she picked up her purse and moved to the door.

"I will find you a wonderful therapist, Mrs. Sloan," I said. I thought, *I had it wrong. She was even more desperate. The loss of her husband decimated her. She no longer had a world. Jimmy represented what remained of her husband, her early parental figures, and G-d knows who.*

She nodded slightly. Indeed, her terror and sense of isolation could be greatly eased by the right person. I made a mental note to call my highly qualified, unusually compassionate colleague, Laura Russell.

After she left, Jimmy turned to me and extended his hand. "Thank you, Dr. Meyers.

His demeanor had changed.

What had happened these past minutes? The storm had broken and light had filled the room. It's never one single thing that moves the patient forward to a place of healing. It's an amalgamation of listening, talking, questioning . . . hoping.

After Jimmy left, I sank into my chair, exhausted. It was then I noticed he had left his cane behind. Sometimes the promise of a breakthrough is only an oasis that turns into a mirage as one draws near. Not today. Today was for real. As my father used to say, "A good day for the Jews."

# FIVE

Years ago in graduate school one of my professors hung a banner across the front of the classroom. In big, bold, handwritten letters it said:

> A hawk has a brain that is 2 x 4 inches in size. A man has a brain that is 8 x 8 inches in size. A hawk will never be anything but a hawk. But a man, a man has choices.

I had closed my eyes for a moment, may have even drifted off, when the memory of that banner flashed before me. I realized how wise my teacher had been to present that deceptively simple fact to us in such a dramatic way.

At Jimmy's age, I'd had no idea what path to choose. The choice I eventually made defined me. And now I was in a good place, in the right profession to help Jimmy realize that there even *was* a choice. His mother would be more difficult. There was much work to do with that odd couple but, for the moment, I felt empowered to face the challenge.

Marine Officer Martin had instructed me to try to fix the souls that had been damaged by the war. Yet infinitely more complex were the seemingly ordinary people damaged by secrets and shame. They were everywhere, living in hell behind their own facades. Only when the facades began to crack could I begin to guide them home.

As I thought of Jimmy and his remarkable breakthrough, I knew that at least one choice I'd made this day had truly paid off. Although I'd wanted to hide after Frank's terrifying call, I had fought off my personal turmoil and continued with my work. As a result, at least those two lost souls would begin a new leg of their journey.

My last scheduled appointment was a consultation with a potential new patient who had called a week before, referred by a colleague. She was due at five o'clock, and promptly there was purposeful knocking on my office door. I let the woman in, noting with relief that Officer Stone was back in the hallway, protecting my life.

Susan Decker greeted me with a firm handshake, clearly a professional woman, impeccably groomed. Tall and elegant, she wore a cobalt blazer over a low-cut blouse, and high heels that emphasized a dancer's calves. Her thick red hair was brushed to a high gloss and bobbed just above her shoulders. Miss Decker could have passed as a fashion model, a doctor or a corporate executive. Whatever her profession, however, it was clear she felt uncomfortable confined in my office.

As she sat, the slit in her skirt opened halfway up her thigh but she made no attempt to rearrange it. Her eyes darted in order not to meet mine. She held her hands in her lap with her fingers entwined and shifted nervously, trying to find a comfortable position. Her breathing was unsteady and she eyed the door as though she wanted to bolt to the nearest bar for a martini to calm her nerves.

I allowed a long moment of "therapist's silence." My practiced ear could "hear" her mind working overtime, figuring out how to begin. She looked down, struggling with increased agitation, so finally I spoke. "Miss Decker, please tell me why you're here."

After a long pause she lifted her eyes to meet mine. They were sapphire blue and full of tears. "I want to speak with you about some things in my life that have gradually accumulated to cause me much discomfort."

"Whatever you want to say, Miss Decker, is confidential and I make no judgments . . . and there is no rush."

"What should I tell you, Doctor? Where do I begin?"

"Wherever you want to begin. I'll jump in with questions as we proceed."

"OK."

Again, I waited.

A look of surprise crossed her face as she suddenly became aware how physically revealing her clothing was. She rearranged her skirt and pulled her blazer jacket around her, perhaps to feel safer.

Finally, she began. "I grew up in Cincinnati. I had no brothers or sisters. My parents were married young—it will be forty years next year. They were good parents if a bit . . . rigid. My dad has worked for Colgate-Palmolive forever and will retire shortly. My mom taught Sunday school—still does—and also teaches private piano lessons.

"I can't say we were ever close. Not distant exactly—more like people sharing a house rather than living as a family. No one drank. We went to church. And truly I can't remember ever having a meaningful fight with my folks while I was growing up."

As I listened I began to sketch a profile. Whatever brought Susan Decker to my door had started long ago with a classic lack of bonding. She looked at me expectantly.

"And?" I said.

"And? You have nothing to say, Doctor?"

"I have some initial thoughts, Miss Blake, but I need to know more about your situation."

She became more uncomfortable, not knowing how to sit or what to say next. Her thighs were once again on full display and she had let go of her blazer and unbuttoned the top of her blouse, fanning herself with her hand. Her eyes met mine. She was looking for a reaction. I offered nothing but my intention to listen carefully. She closed her eyes.

"Well, I remember always being alone. My parents made no effort to involve me in social situations nor did they support me in those things I pursued on my own. Even when I went off to college our relationship remained distant. They only asked that I call them every Sunday evening at six, and I always did so."

"What did you discuss during those calls?"

"The weather, classes, a movie, what I had planned for the week . . ."

"Where?"

"Where?" she repeated.

"Where did you attend college?"

"Northwestern, and then University of Chicago Law. I chose Northwestern because it promised a great many artistic, creative students who could engage emotionally in a way I'd never experienced growing up. And then, law school because I wanted to 'right wrongs,' I guess."

"What wrongs?"

She looked perplexed. "I don't know . . ."

I waited. More fidgeting; then the words came faster.

"The wrongs of a life not lived: well-meaning parents who withheld themselves, a void of sexual relations, dead-end jobs that gave me no satisfaction, feeling sorry for homely friends, even though they had dates and relationships. Shame because I masturbated about boys who didn't know my name or couldn't pick *me* out of line up."

"And yet you're attractive. You must know that?"

She didn't seem to hear me. "I'm here because of shame about the terrible secret that I—"

Here she shifted again, becoming more sexually charged. The transformation was subtle yet astonishing.

"Can you share your feelings about this secret? You're safe here."

"Then it wouldn't be a secret now, would it, Doctor?" She giggled slightly. "If my parents knew I was here they'd join the witness protection program."

"Miss Decker, you're an adult. You're an attractive, articulate woman. Yet the mention of boys, even those in your past, seems to shut you down."

"Doctor, I didn't date boys in high school. And was not interested in the frat brothers in college or law students in grad school."

"There was no one?" I asked.

"Just . . . just one."

Silence, except for my seven little clocks ticking away.

"I finally went out with a guy off campus and had sex for the first time. For some reason I have yet to figure out, we married. Three weeks later we had the marriage annulled. I refused to let him touch me. I thought that if he touched me again my flesh would burn."

"You thought that intimacy, sex, closeness, would burn you like a visit to hell? What a terrible concept to live with," I said.

"He was a good man, and I hurt him deeply."

Her brow furrowed. She took a clip from her purse and piled her glossy hair up and off her neck. She stood and straightened her skirt, and then sat back down. She looked at her nails as if checking a recent manicure. She was a ball of coiled energy, glancing up from time to time to see if I was watching. My eyes never wavered. All at once, she relaxed and was eager to talk.

"Dr. Meyers, I'm thirty-seven years old. I'm a successful attorney here in Manhattan. Six months ago I met a man who wants to marry me and I believe I want to marry him. Yet, if I tell him the truth about my past he will leave me, of that I'm certain."

She closed her eyes and sighed deeply. Then she looked around. The paint hadn't peeled off the walls, the traffic still hummed outside; the furnishings hadn't turned into fire-breathing monsters. She seemed relieved.

"Why don't men have a place in your life?" I asked.

"You're the doctor! That's why I'm here. You tell me."

"It's something we have to discover together. You say you've recently met someone."

"After fourteen years."

My astonishment must have shown.

"Yes! Fourteen long years. After law school I moved to New York, got a good position in a top firm. I'm good at what I do and make lots of money. I have a few girlfriends, mostly co-workers. I've been asked out on dates but have never accepted. Then I met Tim."

There was a long pause. I waited it out.

Finally, "My sex with Tim is pleasant but nothing more. The lights are off, and the relations have a sweet sameness to them. There's no heat, no surprise. I want him to ravage me but I'm afraid to bring it up."

"Why?"

"Why? He'd think I'm a whore."

"Why do you assume he'd think that?"

"Because I *am* a whore," she blurted. "And I hate myself for it!"

"Why do you label yourself so?"

36

She laughed contemptuously and began to breathe more heavily. She uncrossed her legs and leaned forward, suddenly the alpha female.

"For the past two years I've gone to a gangbang club on the Lower East Side."

She seemed keen on shocking me.

"Every Thursday I have sex with strangers—six, seven, eight men at a time. I don't know their names. And don't care what they look like. Other than instructions *from me* as to how to fuck me, in what holes, whether I should eat their cum or have it cover my naked body, no words are exchanged. Some rampant lust takes over and I'm not me. *Me?* That's funny. Who is that anyway?

"Sometimes other women join the group. They too remain nameless and faceless but I let them, in fact encourage them, to do things that are shocking and grotesque. Tie me up! Spank me! Call me horrid names! And through it all I have orgasm after orgasm and through it all I hate the sick deviant I am.

"When my time's finished I get dressed but never shower. I go home covered in semen and the scents of women's vaginas and I don't shower till morning when I get ready for work."

She paused for air.

"So in this way you're not alone," I stated calmly. "The scent of these strangers stays with you all night."

"Didn't you hear what I just said? You have no *judgment* of me?"

"No. Right now you're acting out the frustration of never being able to bond with your parents. You behave in this extreme way because you simply don't want to be trapped alone in a sterile, bland environment. That's why you don't shower following these episodes."

This infuriated her. "No, I'm evil!"

"Have you hurt anyone, or caused anyone physical pain?"

She hesitated, searching for the answer. "No! No . . ." Her eyes searched mine. "But Tim," she whispered. "It would kill him if he knew. Why can't I stop wanting to go to the club? It's danger and divine adrenaline! But if I don't stop I'll lose Tim. He'll think I'm a freak. He'll find me disgusting."

"You must give him the chance to—"

"No! As long as he doesn't know, he sees in me what he wants. I need that. I want to change but I can't."

"You're coming here is a change. Tim is a change."

She looked at me with a ferocity I hadn't seen in her earlier or, for that matter, anyone except in a rare few patients over the years.

"I can't change! I'm a freak!!" Then she shuddered and sobbed uncontrollably.

I waited as the clocks ticked until finally she came back to herself. Then gently I said, "Miss Decker, you're not a freak. You have some issues we need to explore. But you're not a freak."

The sobbing subsided. I knew she was hearing me.

"We'll work this out in safety and find the life force in you. That part of you will always be yours. If Tim is right for you then you'll find that part of him and join to build a strong relationship."

Still shaky, she took out her compact mirror and daubed at her makeup. Despite her tear-streaked face, she looked younger, as though the torturous tale she'd just told was less powerful having escaped her lips. I could hear the shopkeeper below pulling down his security gate.

"It's six o'clock, Miss Decker. I can work you in next Friday at five o'clock."

I held out one of my smaller clocks, which I set to her next appointment time. *Time you cannot take back. It* moves on, relentlessly. Only so much of it to do so very much," all the clocks in the office remind me.

"Keep this in your purse to remind yourself that you're committed to coming back to continue the work we've begun today. And that I'm committed to helping you do that."

She smiled a little. "A Minnie Mouse clock?"

"One has to keep one's sense of humor."

As she took it, our hands touched. "Five o'clock it is."

I felt a twinge of something and was relieved when she turned to go. At the door, she turned back and smiled. Her eyes seemed to search my soul. When the door shut, I could still see them.

# SIX

I packed my briefcase with the files and the notes I'd taken throughout the day. I checked the safety on the .45 Kimber and returned it to my shoulder holster under my sports coat. I turned out the lights, locked the door and walked the hallway.

Officer Stone stood at his post, staring after Miss Decker who was just exiting below. What might he have heard through the closed door of my office? Certainly her sobbing. Might he have overheard the word "gangbang"? After many years hearing people confess their deepest sexual fantasies, I was a somewhat inured soul myself.

"Just another ordinary day," I quipped. He broke character and smiled. Despite his brawn and no-nonsense exterior, the smile made him seem less intimidating and younger.

"Officer Stone, I don't mean to impose nor make light of the threats Mr. Todd made on my life, but would it be possible to escort me home and have someone pick me up early in the morning to appear at the precinct instead of going now? It's been an unusually . . . complicated day. The situation would be better served if I had an early supper, hugged my wife and got some rest."

The man looked at me with curiosity. Life surprises us with its ugliness at times, and then turns on a dime and offers unexpected goodwill.

"My pleasure, Doc. It's been a long day for me too. I'll escort you home and pick you up tomorrow at 7 a.m. to follow up."

I'd been with Grace for twelve years now. We were married shortly after Officer Martin scuttled my dream of becoming a marine. In addition to my half-hearted pushups and red meat eating, I'd been spending my days at a dive on 135th Street, contemplating my future while staring at the bottom of successive Pilsner glasses. Shot glasses filled with a guy named Jack stood at the ready nearby. I never actually drank the whiskey but it was there in case I truly needed to escape my sense of being utterly displaced.

This weeklong pity fest ended one afternoon when a young woman with long raven hair appeared, sat at the stool next to me and said to the barman, "His next round is on me and bring me the same."

I looked up and saw a pretty smile, despite the absence of a tooth above her lower lip. She asked, "Is that all right with you, sweetheart?"

I stared at her for a moment. She was vaguely familiar.

"Sure, thanks. That's very kind of you . . . er . . .?"

"Grace."

"That's very kind of you, Grace."

The barman followed her instructions and when he was done Grace lifted the shot glass and offered a toast.

"Nice to finally meet you, Elias. It's been a long time coming."

She downed the amber liquid in one swallow. I tentatively followed suit. The alcohol burned my throat and filled my loins with warmth. I suppressed a cough and washed down the Jack with a gulp of beer.

"How do you know my name?" I sounded a bit hoarse and felt more than a little flushed.

"I asked around the past couple of days. I mean, I had

my eye on you when you were on campus and then you disappeared and I wondered who chased you away."

Her eyes danced with intelligence. "So why did you go and what brought you back, Mr. Elias?"

Was she actually flirting with me? Me? Invisible Elias, just Elias? I concentrated on sounding sober.

"My demons, my lack of a road map and . . ." I have no idea why I added, "And because the Marines said I'm a wimp!"

Grace threw her head back and laughed. "Then you're the cutest wimp I've ever met!" She put her arm around my waist and pulled me close, making sure I felt her breasts against my chest. Then her hand found its way to my ass, where it lingered.

"Thank you, barman, we'll be leaving now." She threw a couple of bills on the counter.

I was a little unsteady on my feet. "Grace, what do you want with me? I mean, I don't even have a tattoo."

"No tattoo!" she exclaimed in mock surprise. "I don't believe it. I'll have to examine you and see for myself. I hope you're not modest."

"Modest?" I slurred a little. "No, I'm just a wimp who needs to do some more pushups. Modesty is not in my vocabulary. Neither is 'private.' I'm just a marine reject. I drink here alone and for the record I don't usually drink."

"Silly. You're not drinking alone. You're with me now and we're leaving."

"Where are we going?" I swayed slightly.

"My place—to see if we can find that hidden tattoo."

She took my hand and led me into the sunshine.

Grace lived just a couple of blocks from the bar in which she had tracked me down. In fact, I discovered quickly that I had been on her radar for some time now as my studio apartment was just around the corner from her student housing complex.

We walked hand in hand. My feet scarcely touched the ground.

"Are you sure you don't have me confused with some other guy?" I ventured.

Again that lusty, uninhibited laugh.

"No, seriously," I protested. "You could have any guy. Why me?"

She looked at me with gentle intensity. "Because you're adorable; because you have beautiful eyes; because you're so smart. I never missed a class in Comparative Psychology because whenever you answered a question I found it, what? Well, inspiring. No one speaks like that without having written it down first! And smart is my aphrodisiac. And you're Jewish and my family doesn't like the Jews so perhaps my desire for you is some sort of rebellion. What do you think?"

"I don't know," I replied. "The last thing I heard you say was 'my desire for you.'"

"Well, we'll figure it out together," she said.

Even though Grace was taller than me, she made me feel as though I matched her height. G-d she was beautiful! Dark, almost jet-black hair with a slight wave framed a pale, perfect complexion, her bright, brown eyes full of humor. Through her sweater were breasts like those I'd only seen in *Playboy* and imagined in my dreams. Her legs were long and shapely, and as she walked her athletic posterior moved ever so slightly from side to side. She was animated and fun, blatantly available and it seemed she had chosen me.

We had reached the front door of her building.

"Are you ready for me to find that hidden tattoo of yours?" she asked with mischief in her eyes.

"You can look but don't think you'll find one."

"Well if that's true, we'll just have to figure out something else to do."

She opened the door and invited me in. I entered and she closed the door behind me.

My life changed forever.

# SEVEN

Grace and I were wow in the sack. When naked she seemed to morph into an Aphrodite sex goddess. She found pleasure in pleasuring me and I discovered her hot buttons with willing guidance from her. It was like an endless rollercoaster ride—crazy abandon, surprises galore and you never had to get off and pay another nickel! She looked long and hard for that phantom tattoo. And it was wonderful.

Grace was studying to be a sex therapist, living on the cheap to make it through school by working two waitress jobs, as diligent about her studies and goals as I had once been. We were a threesome: her studies, my devotion, and a roaring love affair that made us inseparable. The slow revelation that I should go back to school and get a PhD gradually lifted the bell jar off my future. The sky became bluer, the moon glowed with magic, and food from the sidewalk vendor tasted like dinner at the Ritz and the sex was off the charts.

After a couple of months, we married. Her vaguely anti-Semitic mother thought Grace must be with child, gossip was rampant and the family could scarcely contain their contempt for me throughout our non-denominational ceremony. My parents had been distant since I had left the nest. If my marrying a non-Jew disturbed them, they didn't show it openly, although they made a point of sitting in the far reaches of the chapel.

Ten months after the wedding, our first child was born, and whatever hostilities that might have simmered between our divergent families ended with oohs and aahs over the crib. We became one big stew of religion, philosophy, and recipes, uneasily united by blood.

Life seemed like an open, sunny field. Yet a deep melancholy hung over my new wife from time to time. Any marriage, even the most blessed, hits speed bumps. The daily grind brews subtle resentments and it's common for ardor to cool. But I was determined to ferret out the source of her pain.

I had assumed that Grace's father was deceased, but one night, after some wine and sex, I learned that he had actually abandoned the family when she was fifteen. She grew up believing that he left because he wanted nothing to do with her once she had a boyfriend. His betrayal was somehow her fault.

She was born in the Bronx on the Grand Concourse—in its pre-war days, the apex of good American living. It was indeed grand, with tall, well-appointed buildings flanking the wide boulevard that seemed to never end. Grace's mother worked a grueling assortment of jobs as did Grace's older sister. Life was a struggle but respectable.

Eager to be the protector of my new wife, I set out on a quixotic mission to help her find answers about her father, closure of some sort. However, I was a detective with scant clues. Fortunately, after a few drinks Grace's mother went into a rambling discourse about the evil James Madden.

"He was a big man. He'd take me out in the winter cold for long walks when we first met and in the summer on sailing trips. He liked to sail. At the time I thought he was sweet, but once he left us I knew he was never what he seemed. Everything he did or said was a lie."

Her sister was even more vitriolic when I broached the subject. The only solid lead was that he had been a trucker at a place called The Hauling Company in the Bronx. He had finally risen to a management position in dispatch—then disappeared.

I made an appointment with Stephen Marx, the current manager of the company, a tall man in his late forties who had left Germany before the war. Making his way to America, he had enlisted in the Marines to prove his patriotism. Although he resembled Santa Claus, with his full head of white hair and beard, he carried a certain aura of darkness as if he had seen too much action in battle.

When I introduced myself, he offered his hand with an inquisitive smile that crinkled his eyes and lifted his eyebrows. But when I told him I was looking for James Madden, his eyes became furtive and a flash of anger crossed his face. He withdrew his hand quickly.

"Madden?" he said. "Gone long before I arrived. Never met the man. Sorry, big shipment due any minute." He rushed away and then turned back. "But trust me, you're looking for someone you don't really want to find."

I stood for a moment, dumbfounded.

There were framed photos of the early trucks and their drivers hanging on his office walls. Grace's dad must have been close to seventy and might even be dead by now. What had he done to make a war vet as tough as Marx shudder and run at the mention of his name? If I found James Madden would it lead to anything good? Would it ease the feelings of abandonment and guilt my young bride had carried since she was a child? Madden was a potentially dangerous man and I was a therapist, not a detective. But I had committed myself to the mission.

I left the office, walked away from the commercial section of the Bronx toward the Grand Concourse and jumped a train to the Military Recruiting Station in Times Square. Madden had served in WWII. It would be a good place to start. The office in New York and another in Washington housed the records of thousands of soldiers who had fought in both wars.

I was greeted by a stern young marine and explained my situation. Once he heard the story, his demeanor changed. Coincidentally, his father had also deserted him when he was an infant, leaving him with a brokenhearted mom in rural Tennessee. He left the counter and disappeared into an office. Some twenty minutes later he reappeared and beckoned for me to join him.

I entered a huge room filled with hundreds of filing cabinets and a single long, pockmarked table. He had pulled a huge eleven-by-fourteen-inch leather-bound book. It was opened to the name James Madden, The Bronx NY.

"This appears to be your guy, Doctor," he whispered. "Take a look, but you can't stay long. I shouldn't even let you back here. So read fast!" I did.

James Madden, b. 1905, was the munitions officer for the 18th Infantry Regiment in the Battle of Crucifix Hill led by Captain Bobbie Bowen, that took place on October 8th, 1944 near the village of Haaren in Germany. Their mission was to gain control of the hill, which was laced with a maze of pillboxes and bunkers so that surrounding the German Volksgrenadierdivision would be complete.

As the leading rifle platoon of C Company assaulted the first pillbox, flanking fire from a nearby pillbox took the platoon in crossfire. The pinned-down soldiers experienced an intense artillery barrage on their exposed positions, sustaining many casualties.

With his men dying around him, Captain Bobbie Bowen, the company commander, grabbed a pole charge and ran 100 yards with bullets whipping by him and placed it into the pillbox, destroying it. He did this twice more. With Madden's help, he destroyed two more. During the third effort, he was gravely wounded by a mortar round but refused medical attention until the mission was complete. Madden dragged him down the hill to safety. He recovered but was severely handicapped. Captain Bobbie Bowen was awarded the Medal of Honor and James Madden received an honorable discharge. Captain Bowen took his own life on January 17th of 1948.

Some demons never leave you. I noticed the date of the Captain's suicide. It was more than a coincidence that Grace's father ran away some three weeks later. Could the two events be connected?

The next day I returned to see Mr. Marx at The Hauling Company and waited a long while for a man who clearly didn't want to see me. As the clock reached six, I blocked him as he left his office.

"Mr. Marx, please, sir, a minute of your time?" I asked firmly. Marx looked at me as if he had just eaten a lemon but he did indeed stop in his tracks.

"What? What do you want from me? I told you Madden was long gone when I began working here."

"Yes, sir, I know, but I have just one question."

"If I have an answer I'll give it to you. If not, I don't want to see you here again. Is that understood?"

"Yes," I said. "Is there any record of driving accidents during Mr. Madden's last weeks as a dispatcher here?"

He went ghost white. "Indeed," he whispered. "It remains the only blemish on the company's proud history. Madden sent a young driver out in a blizzard, knowing the roads would be unmanageable, and he did so despite the fact there was no urgency to the delivery." He stopped.

"What happened, sir?"

"The poor kid couldn't handle the roads—the ice, the wind—and veered off the highway to his death. Due to the weather back then in February of '48 they couldn't get to the truck for days, and when they did, the contents were gone, the truck was empty and the driver frozen at the wheel."

"And what was taken from the truck?" I asked, already suspecting the answer.

"Munitions," he replied. "He sent a good man out to die. He killed that poor driver same as shooting him in the chest."

"My G-d!" I was beginning to put the pieces together. "Was there an investigation?"

"Madden disappeared. Now, don't ask me no more about him. I done told you what I know about that fella. Maybe you're smart enough to figure out why—the police weren't. I say he was a demon."

So Captain Bowen was awarded the Medal of Honor and Madden received an honorable discharge. Shortly after the war ended, Bowen took his own life. A short time later, Madden disappeared. For me it all began to line up.

Grace's dad had been a munitions officer in a traumatizing situation. His comrade in arms had escaped his battered body and unspeakable memories by committing suicide. Madden was overwhelmed with the pressure of an expanding family and needed to find a way out. Finally, the chance presented itself. He ordered a deadly ride into whiteout conditions, waited for the inevitable, and then arranged to sell the contents of the truck on the black market in order to make the money to leave his family behind. He got his freedom at the cost of a man's life and the devastation of his own family.

Where did he go? He ran without leaving a note or a dollar, but where did he go? My only leads were that he liked the cold, he liked to sail, and he had no moral compass. So, I figured, he might have wound up in Maine or New Hampshire or even in Vermont—all places with cold, blue sailing waters.

The following weekend, I made my first stop Burlington, Vermont, and checked in at the postal office. Perhaps I should have chosen a career as a private investigator instead of a shrink, for there he was in black and white on the town register: Captain James Madden, 3411 Lake Rd. Not even an alias, which demonstrated his blatant arrogance. Any good psychopath should know to cover his tracks.

I took a taxi to the address. There it was, right on the mailbox, in handwritten cursive, "The Maddens." I asked the taxi driver to wait. He agreed for a ten spot. Suddenly I felt weak in the knees. I was about to meet Grace's long-lost father.

The house was small, with a carefully manicured landscape that was ablaze with the colors of summer. Voices came from the backyard and I walked toward them. There he was! I knew it at once; the resemblance was uncanny. A sailboat was docked nearby, abutting the porch, and seated next to him was a woman who must have been thirty years younger. Lucky girl, I thought. Married an older man who would surely pass before she would. And she would never know about those he cheated and left behind. In this case her ignorance was her bliss.

When I called his name, he stood abruptly and looked down on me from the porch with wary eyes.

"Who are you?" he barked.

"I'm your daughter Grace's husband. My name is Elias Meyers."

He jutted out his chin and stood taller as if ready for a fight and turned to his young wife. "Go inside, dear. I have to talk to this man."

She was reluctant but did as she was told, never taking her eyes off me until she was safe inside, with the sliding glass door closed behind her.

He looked at me hard. "I don't have no daughter, fella, so unless you're looking for trouble I suggest you clear the hell out. You're trespassing!"

"Look, Madden, I know who you are and what you've done. I didn't come here to fuck things up any further . . ."

"Then why did you come, Mr. Meyers?"

"It's Dr. Meyers." Suddenly I was seething. "I came because I promised your daughter I'd find you, to see if you would like to meet something precious you left behind, replace some of your shame with the pride of knowing that despite your kicking her to the curb like a piece of shit, your daughter turned out to be a fantastic woman!"

He recoiled a little and then glanced nervously toward the house. The curtain moved slightly. He came down the steps and moved closer.

"I don't need to see her, even if she is my daughter. You got no proof. Maybe her mama was sleepin' around . . ."

I could smell his foul breath.

"You're some kike, aren't you? I can see it in them beady eyes. You come out of nowhere, tell me I was bad for leaving? You know nothing about me! Go judge someone else and leave me in peace, or I'll get my gun!"

The thought of my wife filled me with power. "You're a sorry excuse for a human being, Madden. I can see that Grace is better off never meeting you. In fact, she'd be better off if you were dead and that's what I plan to tell her. You'll live the rest of your days with the fear I saw behind your eyes a few minutes ago. Someday your young wife will bundle you off to a nursing home. And then you'll die and go to hell. No one will miss you. That's your legacy!"

# EIGHT

Grace found some sort of closure once she learned that her father had drowned in a fishing accident on a lake in upstate New York shortly after he left. "See," I told her, "he probably intended to return. Maybe the shock of hearing about Captain Bowen's suicide made him snap temporarily. Fight or flight syndrome."

I don't think her mother bought it, but nobody ever mentioned James Madden again.

Our lives brightened and we became great partners. I helped her with her graduate studies. She was a great sounding board for the difficult cases that came my way. After Spencer was born, we shared parenting duties, way ahead of our time. But by the time he was two, it was apparent that something was wrong. He was abnormally restless, jumping from one activity to the next, flying into rages unprovoked. Gradually it dawned on me that he might have Attention Deficit Disorder.

Medication was not recommended for such a young child so our lives revolved around his needs, trying to apply any behavior techniques we could learn. We lost babysitter after babysitter, yet somehow it brought us closer, like partners in crime fighting for our child.

When Grace found out she was pregnant again, I was overjoyed. Difficult as it is having an infant, the joy of having a normal baby would balance out our lives. That proved untrue. Rodney, too, had ADD, although it was a milder case. He was quiet, drifted away into imagination, wasn't prone to anger. The strain of the two diverse kids frayed our relationship. On some deep level, I think we blamed each other for our misfortune.

By the time Spencer was six and in a special school, I ran a very large clinic with three thousand patients and four hundred therapists. Grace often worked part time on projects that came in. We were able to have more contact, but always under stress, and we were rarely alone. Grace was increasingly upset with me. I worked too much. I was never around except to sleep and have sex. Gradually, she made me feel inadequate (Impossible. She may have reawakened my feelings of inadequacy, which I always fled from, and here it reared its ugly head. More analytic work for me—uh oh). It seemed I was always wrong, whether it was to do with putting the kids to bed or taking out the trash.

After I became an intern in a private practice, I saw her even less. She seemed to lose interest in her children. I was becoming their mother as well as their father, chief bottle washer and pack horse. And, to complicate matters, Grace was like a teenager with money. I never knew where it went and she became angry when I broached the subject. I was paying the bills, doing the shopping and working fifty to sixty hours a week. And yet I loved her so much, I soldiered on. The flashes of passion, her humor and occasional generosity kept the dysfunctional relationship afloat. I was investing 100% and receiving a 10% return, but she was somehow still my Grace.

Then there was an incident that jolted me to my senses. At a graduation ceremony at NYU, there was to be a major achievement award announced. It was my job to be master of the ceremony, and this event was not scheduled in my plans. Even I, one of the people who had arranged the ceremony, had no idea to whom the award would be granted. This was a closely guarded secret known only to the Chairman of the Board of Trustees.

When he announced the winner, I heard my name and was almost too floored to walk to the podium, so over-whelmed I could scarcely find the words to accept such a coveted honor. If only Grace had known! She would have so enjoyed being there to share the victory.

Then Lillian, the administrative manager, approached to congratulate me. "I definitely thought I'd see your wife here today." In response to my bewildered look she added, "I did call Grace to tell her you'd been selected this year." I was flabbergasted. I mumbled something about Grace's fighting "a touch of flu," and escaped to the men's room. My wife had knowingly failed me.

# NINE

Saturday morning, Officer Stone's cruiser was waiting outside my door promptly at 7 a.m. the morning after the death threat. His uniform was crisp and starched and he greeted me with a warm smile, black coffee and a glazed donut.

The sweet, pungent scent of last night's rain filled the air. The world was fresh and clean; the spring sun was just making its appearance. With each passing moment lights flicked off in the tenement apartments that lined the street. The coffee was hot, the donut still warm, and my protector rode beside me.

He told me what to expect when we met with the sergeant downtown at the precinct. I'd report the incident and my concerns. Most likely, I would have to file an additional complaint at Frank Todd's borough of residence in Prospect Park, Brooklyn. With not much more to say, Stone and I made small talk about city politics, how he liked his job and how I found my way to mine.

There was not much traffic at such an early hour. The streets were coming alive as if in a time-lapse photo: vendors selling coffee and paperboys hawking the morning news. A stick ball game was being played on an asphalt playground near the high school and I remembered being their age and the day I hit a "pinky" out over the twenty-foot fence that surrounded the urban diamond, ending the game.

A big bruiser was at bat and he hit one deep into the sunshine, but it curved foul. Then he laid into one and it sailed over the fence like a rocket with height to spare, smashing against Stone's window with a bang. He slammed on the brakes, as did the car behind us. As the ball bounced away, we looked at each other and shared a sigh of relief. The kids at the fence were hollering for us to retrieve their ball. Stone had just opened the door when a man jumped onto the hood from the passenger side. Frank Todd raised a tire iron and shattered the windshield. As Stone recoiled, Todd punched him. Stone's foot accidentally hit the pedal and we swerved into a sanitation truck idling on the corner. His head hit the dashboard and he was out.

Somehow Todd held on. He was kneeling now, staring down at me through the broken glass. "Now it's your turn, you kike bastard. You fucked with my life, now I'm ending yours."

He pulled out a bowie knife that had been tucked into his trousers and waved it back and forth, grinning from ear to ear—demonstrating its murderous potential. As a psychotherapist I knew he was moving slowly in the hope that I would beg for my life. What he unwittingly gave me were a few precious moments, and in those few moments I reached for my .45 Kimber Ultra, resting in its holster under my sports coat. Upon seeing my pistol, he screamed and reared back. With an almost spastic jerk, I shot him twice in the chest. The third bullet hit the weapon he wielded. The impact caused it to smash against his face with such force his face became a mask of blood. His dead body balanced itself for a moment and then fell across the hood of the white cruiser.

In a heartbeat, the peaceful spring morning had been shattered. "If you attempt to kill, be prepared to die," was a saying my father had taught me. Just then the school bell rang and the kids pressed against the school fence reluctantly headed for class. Shaking like a leaf, I returned the gun to its holster and listened as police sirens filled the air, arriving *en masse*, their blue strobe lights flickering on the still-damp morning pavement. Surreal. Throughout it all my coffee, still in the holder, had not spilled a drop.

# TEN

A battalion of men in blue surrounded the damaged cruiser. Stone lay in an ambulance where two EMS guys had patched him up. I was relieved to see he was partially sitting, giving an initial statement to a number of detectives.

The result of the aborted attempt on my life was spattered all over my clothes. I watched myself as I would watch any patient. Calm and lucid for now thanks to a chain of defense mechanisms, willing my way past the shock. I would carry on and, once at the office, I would change into the extra clothes I kept there. I would process the tragedy and move past it. I was in an "as-if" state. I had never actually shot anything but paper and clay pigeons. I was in total shock and did not recognize it. I just knew I had to go back to work. (So much for all my analysis.)

A crowd was gawking at me, knowing I was a participant in the events that rocked the morning. It made me uncomfortable, actually more so than the fact that I had just shot someone. I gave my report several times to a gaggle of detectives all earnest and stern faced. I turned in my gun to CSU, signed papers for the NYPD, was examined by EMS and saw the ME confirm that Todd was dead and that Stone had been taken to the ER. There were enough letters floating around in my brain for a good scrabble game.

I assured the officer in charge that I was all right and that I would stop by the precinct at the end of my day. He wished me luck, shook my hand and I was released.

I had to get to my office. I had scheduled a few spillover weekend appointments. On an ordinary workday, I would take the subway downtown. It was faster and cheaper than a taxi, but this morning, covered in blood, I felt the need to hide. I held out my hand for a cab, climbed in quickly and gave the driver my address and rolled down the window to let the breeze wash away the morning.

I was a doctor. My life was dedicated to healing people and yet I had just shot someone. "And what do you feel about that?" I asked myself. Shockingly, I felt very little. No regret. No sense of guilt. My only concern was that I felt nothing. That, I found alarming. I had been frightened yesterday morning by the man's threats, yet when he attempted to carry them out I had responded as if I were a trained killer.

My days were filled with stories of woe, mixed up minds and tales of people who had lost their way and I was the only "map" that might get them home safely. Had I become inured to my own feelings in order to function? My concern for my patients and their pain was what drove me, what allowed me to fight through it all with the hope of remedy. Hope and defiance in the face of discontent or something worse. Every day. You had to own courage to do what I did to earn a buck. Nevertheless, I needed to look in the mirror and see who I had become and where I was headed. "Physician, heal thyself."

As we drove downtown the landscapes changed every ten or twelve blocks. There were mean streets, harsh and bare. Spring was omnipresent in the dogwood trees and endless azaleas that lined the affluent neighborhoods. Midtown offered the sterile flash of steel skyscrapers and the large display windows of NY high-end shopping, offering expensive delights for those fortunate to be able to afford them. The city was at full bore now. Well-groomed, suited men walked to work with purpose and pretty woman sashayed in spring garb, attracting the attention of those lingering over a smoke or grabbing a coffee before beginning their day. I felt as though I was in a movie reel, with each new section of town a different scene.

All these people, all this energy. The thousands of faces, each projecting a different story. Triumph. Eagerness. Loss. Sadness. Smiles of promise or flirtation. Expectation. Who were these "everyman" and how many of them carried with them the confusion or desperation that my patients brought to my office?

Less than an hour ago a man intended to slice my face like a slab of bacon. I knew about his demons, perhaps was party to the loss he faced as his wife chose to leave him. Was I, then, responsible for his actions? Could I really save anyone or was I part of making things worse? I felt light-headed.

The taxi pulled to a stop in front of my office. I paid the fare and gave the driver a tip. Then, just before he drove on, I offered him a second tip. "Be happy, my friend. Life is short. Enjoy your day." And then I went to work. I realized my greatest joy was work, then free time, then my wife, my sons, and daughter—then the safe world.

# ELEVEN

I washed up in the small side sink in the back of the office and changed clothes. Then I studied myself closely in the small mirror. I had taken a life.

During WWII I had carried a Gene Autry revolver. My mother and I often walked to the Navy yard where shore patrol Marines and Navy guarded the perimeter. I could hear their bugles from the ships and awoke every morning at 5 a.m. with the armed forces blocks away. My uncles practiced shooting in the basement, weekly preparing for the Nazi invasion. We would not be taken alive, whatever that meant.

Were a bagel and a smear a reasonable breakfast after shooting a man? It had already started to seem like a distant dream. I found half of the bagel I had brought to work yesterday. I had shoved it in my drawer after Frank Todd's call. It was stale but incredibly delicious. Nettie, my first analytic supervisor, always enjoyed stale rolls dunked in hot coffee as we worked. It brought me to my feelings of closeness with her during our year of supervision. She wanted to keep in contact and asked me to start an independent clinic with her and some colleagues. I withdrew from her, too afraid of my own warm emotions to her.

It was eight o'clock and I opened the door to the day's first appointment. A handsome, well-dressed man in his mid thirties waited outside my office. He was reading the sports page of the *Daily News*, leaning casually against the wall.

Ethan Clark wore a perfectly fitted glen-plaid suit, buffed black wing tips, a pastel blue shirt and a pink tie that matched the pocket square that was folded perfectly in place. He had a naturally brooding expression, deep, dark eyes and jet-black hair crisply parted and held in place by a pungent hair gel.

As I unlocked the door he folded the paper and mentioned how disappointingly the Yankees were doing. Entering, he immediately selected the club chair, which was the option closest to me, and jumped right in.

"Doctor, I believe my partner is stealing from me. And a lot. I mean thousands or more every week. And I think he's cooking the books and taking money in cash for his own account."

I listened but had no questions for the moment.

"We have a large garment company. We make mid-priced dresses and sell to all the big stores; you know, Macy's, Lord and Taylor, Saks. I'm the front guy, the salesman. I run the showroom, hire the models, schmooze the clients; he runs the business—money, insurance. And the fucker is stealing from me. I put him on the map and he's picking my pocket!"

"Why see a sex therapist? It sounds like you should be talking to the police rather than someone like me."

"I was told you knew about human nature and could help; and it's not just about the money . . . It does involve some sexual situations as well."

He was clearly distraught, got up from the club chair and paced while wringing his hands. Outside there was a fender bender: first the squeal of tires and the blaring horns, and then the crushing of metal and sounds of shattered glass.

Interesting how life reflects the moment.

He sat again, this time as far from me as possible, and stared at his shiny shoes.

"Have you confronted your partner about your concerns?" I asked.

"They're not concerns, Doctor, they're g-ddamn facts!"

"If you're so certain then why allow it to continue?"

"Because it will blow up my life." His voice filled with petulant defeat.

"Blow up your life? That is indeed a dilemma."

"You have no idea. You have no fucking idea!"

"Quite true," I said. "I can only *imagine* what's going on, which is not the way I like to work."

"So why am I here if you can't help me?"

Trying to calm this anxious, troubled man I answered slowly and softly. "I didn't say I couldn't help you. I said I don't like to imagine the details of your situation. I need to hear the facts, your concerns, and then reflect a bit."

It took him a moment to digest my words and then he revealed his core issue.

"I'm married. And I have five women I see on the side—my mistresses. I enjoy the variety but it's not cheap, and if I confront this guy, Frankie, he'll use it against me. My income might take a hit and I would have to give up some of the girls. Now do you see the problem?"

"Several problems," I replied.

"What? What else do you see?"

"Mr. Clark, you have a partner who you are certain is stealing from you and you are taking no action because you're afraid of blackmail. He might steal more and give you less in exchange for silence. And if that does happen you won't be able to continue to see five girlfriends *and* your wife. For the moment that's enough."

"Why? What do you mean 'for the moment'?"

"Well, your situation sounds like a hand grenade which at any moment could blow up. But by doing nothing you're allowing yourself to be a victim."

"A victim? Does having five girlfriends sound like I'm a victim? And my wife is a dish. I'm happy. I'm no victim."

"Really?"

"Really, what?"

"You don't seem happy. In fact, you're quite distraught. You project as someone who is about to 'lose it.' It being everything."

"What do I do? What do I DO?"

I sat still, quiet. "Mr. Clark, please take a moment to breathe. You came to see me so I might help you. You've been here for just a few minutes. Take a seat. Get comfortable and let's see where it all leads. OK?"

He nodded animatedly.

"Does your wife know about these relations with five other women?"

"Yes, of course. I wouldn't cheat on Holly. I love her. She's my wife. Why would you ask such a question?"

"Can't imagine," I said. Happily, my sarcasm was lost on him.

I began reflecting on what he had said. This guy couldn't be this stupid, could he? They say "G-d takes care of children, drunks and fools." Ethan Clark clearly had G-d's ear. Was he in denial? Was he so weak as to allow this abuse from his partner? Five women *and* an accommodating wife!

"Mr. Clark, when do you have time to see all these women and your wife?"

He looked at me as if I had just put ketchup on a fifty-dollar-steak at The Palm.

"I see my wife every Saturday into Sunday evening. I see the other woman on a regular schedule as they all have a specific night. Missy and Blake are sisters so I see them on the same night. Not a problem," he said triumphantly.

"Well, that's good!" I said.

"It is. Everyone's happy."

"Except you, Mr. Clark. Except you."

He appeared ready to challenge my remark but stopped short of speaking. Instead he stood quickly and then all the energy left his body and he collapsed on the couch and put his face in his hands.

"That's true, everyone is happy but me. Everyone but me." He took his hands away and his face was flushed and his eyes filled with confusion.

"Mr. Clark," I said, "I think we have to start by my meeting your wife. We have to be on a solid foundation here, and I need to hear her say she's fine with these mistresses . . ."

"Sure if that helps." He was suddenly alive with hope.

"It's a place to start. I do take appointments on Saturday and have time tomorrow early afternoon, if that works for you."

"Sure, of course, Holly and I will be here. On time. What time?"

"Two."

"Wonderful, Doctor. Thank you. So much. You're a life saver. See you tomorrow. And let's hope the Yankees can win tonight."

"OK. Let's hope. See you tomorrow." Mixed priorities, I thought.

After he left I needed a chance to contemplate the state of affairs. I made myself a pot of coffee and sat on the windowsill looking down at the street. There were police cars and cops sorting out the crash I had heard earlier during the session with Clark. Dome lights flickered and indecipherable commands were thrown around. Before too long those in charge would have it all in order.

"Order" was a word not used often in my profession, and I felt a small pang of jealousy that it wasn't part of my vocabulary. The street was aglow under the spring sun. Yet two dented cars stood at odd, opposing angles, their owners glum on opposite street corners. A dichotomy.

The phone rang and I picked up on the second ring.

"Dr. Meyers, it's Jimmy Sloan."

It sounded like a stronger man than the Jimmy I had been treating.

"Yes, Jimmy, how are you?"

"I'm fine," he said tentatively. "I just called to tell you that my mother attempted to kill herself last night. She used a gun. It appears she'll be all right but I just thought you should know."

"Jimmy, I'm so sorry. Do you need to see me today?"

"No, I'm fine. Just wanted you to know. I just wanted you to know," he repeated. "I'll see you at our regular scheduled time. Stay well, Doctor."

Suicide? Clark had just left telling me that I was a "life saver." Apparently, not true. Todd was gone and now Phyllis Sloan had tried to follow. But thank G-d she'd failed. I made a mental note to call Laura, a therapist who might better help Jimmy's mother.

I continued to gaze out the window and sipped my coffee. How did I get to this place? I had raced through schools, clinics and into private practice. I was a Jewish kid who was driven to succeed, whose goal ten years ago was to make serious money. I enjoyed my work—well, in reality I was fascinated by it. It didn't often bring enjoyment.

Yet I knew I was gifted. I had developed an approach that had saved a great many people. However, my life was less and less my own. I shared it with a gaggle of troubled souls whose woe I carried with me every day. And I had begun to lose part of myself in their stories. Was it my home life that needed work or was it the work I did that affected my life at home?

Maybe I needed to see my own shrink to figure that one out. I helped people. My days mattered and so did I. Many couldn't say that about themselves. And although my days were difficult and sometimes confusing, I would continue to practice and become better at my craft. Clouds had swept in and obfuscated the sun, the sky had darkened quickly, there was a clap of thunder and it began to rain.

# TWELVE

June Hurley was a black widow in every sense of the word, except she didn't eat her prey. Unlike real spiders that were merely acting out preprogrammed behavior, June chose to live her life without remorse or morality, ignoring the consequences of her actions. Many in my field believe that substance, character and behavior are formed within the first thirty months of our lives. Human beings become stunted if we grow up lacking love and are not taught by example what remorse and accountability are. Sometimes behavior is simply misguided and we act out in small ways but deep down we are "healthy."

With others, the acting out becomes dark, violent or psychotic. Those whose narcissism transcends all else leave carnage in their wake. Their victims lie prone and unsuspecting as the poisonous venom enters them. And the Black Widow relishes it all. It's her game, her thrill, to overwhelm their life force. And she never fails. Well, almost never.

June could have passed for thirty in the dim light of a club. Despite her actual age, just shy of fifty, she remained stunning "even under the bright lights of a hotel bathroom," she boasted often during our sessions. She was amoral and wore it proudly. Her mantra was, "You fucked me; what did you expect? Love? I never promised you anything but hot sex and if you pine for more of the same, then pay up!"

The more men pursued her, the more she toyed with their affections. They wanted love as did she, but her issues caused changes of those feelings. Although she was desperately lonely for a heart that would beat next to hers, she lacked the capacity to let one in. So she remained angry and alone.

The source of June's condition was a broken, dysfunctional home and a mother who married three times. When she was an adolescent, already in a confusing stage of development, her mother got back together with June's father and then moved away with him, killing her one chance to take back what she missed out on as a child.

Once we enter adulthood with its accompanying pressures—work, family, and the like—it's increasingly difficult to prevent neurosis from being cemented into the personality. That's why therapy takes time, commitment. For a time, I thought June was up for the task. Then I realized that she was having too much fun fulfilling her appetite. June's men, her victims, struggled in vain, trying to find ways to keep her, even as she moved on to the next.

June had been married five times, using her physical assets as a way to entrap her men. But once the heat of each honeymoon had cooled, she created such chaos and so much angst that each husband in succession gave her a small fortune to go away. She justified her actions, believing that whatever her spouses did for her had never been good enough. June beat the foolish men into the turf. She felt no remorse, as she had never loved. She enjoyed the game because she was ill, and netted fiscal revenge for love not gotten. We worked hard together, but just as she was on the verge of being able to define her neurosis, she met fellow therapist Dr. Walter Brennan in a bar one night and regressed.

She began to spend every Friday night with middle-aged Dr. Brennan, a married man with three children all in college, and a wife whom he hadn't touched in years. June proudly said, "If you asked his wife why on earth she stays with Walter she'd say, 'Because if I divorce him I might lose this house and I love my house.'" June thought that was hilarious.

Walter was a sex therapist to the rich and famous. He worked minimal hours, but to see him you needed a reference and had to be willing to go onto an endless waiting list. For easy access you paid his "emergency fee" of $1200 an hour. He had lost any shred of integrity long ago and was . . . what? A completely narcissistic douche bag. Walter didn't turn women like June on with his looks, which were pasty and bland, or his charm—he was devoid of that. Rather he did it with money, a calculating heart, and a lack of morals. So once he met June, he was in Shangri-La. Three years of hot, discrete sex that didn't threaten his "home life," a charade he perpetuated in the bedroom community of Great Neck just fourteen miles from his Park Avenue office.

A normal Friday night date would begin with an expensive dinner at the St. Regis, the Four Seasons or the Park Lane. He'd talk and June would listen sympathetically. His work had become mundane; every patient seemed hopeless. Long ago, he had lost his ardor for healing others; now it was about money. June would commiserate with his woe, nod appropriately and then take him upstairs and fuck him. Not in the missionary position; in everything but.

She let him tie her up and degrade her sexually. He'd demand she demean herself by calling herself a slut and shout out how much she needed his cock. She begged him to punish her sexually, to hurt her, to leave her in physical pain, under the mask of rough sex. She would then scream in honest pain, not acting, when he manhandled her groin, anus, and breasts, causing perverse pleasure for him. He was in control and that is what "got him off."

It didn't hurt that June was a Rubenesque sexpot with white, unblemished skin, large, perfect breasts and a round Botero ass that stood to attention. All available and accompanied by a chorus of moans and screams of ecstasy. Dr. Brennan was a sadist made more frightening by the fact that June was pliable and unaware of the damage his behavior was inflicting on her psyche. He treated her like scum and chipped away at whatever self-esteem she still possessed. In return she became richer than she had ever imagined.

Now nearing fifty, with her nubile years waning, she was wise enough to know that, soon, dim lights would not shield her from years of excessive alcohol—that the Black Widow would lose her power to seduce. So one night, after Walter had his way with her and fucked her like a bitch in heat, she proposed a plan. He actually listened and was not averse at all—actually enthusiastic, once he had her assurance that he could still have her at his beck and call. To prove her loyalty, the following Friday he arranged for three younger men to fuck her all at once while he watched and orchestrated everyone's actions. When she complied, he was convinced.

As for June, she kept reminding herself that she could bear anything for thirty minutes. ANYTHING. She would always survive no matter what her "lovers" did to her. The experience reaffirmed her belief that there were no good men and that no man would ever save her. On Saturday morning, after she had passed Walter's test, she barked the orders and he obeyed.

During her time with Walter, she had discovered that there were many doctors like him who were indifferent to their patients—bored, jaded and corrupt. As a prestigious therapist, Walter had contacts with a number of them who had clients who wanted high-end ganja and designer drugs. He agreed to provide the drugs for June to sell, along with her body, to the lost and horny in need of an unbridled high. He would arrange the initial meetings for her through his cronies and they would all split the profits.

His one reservation was that in the small world of New York therapists there were a few old-line therapists who still held onto their ethics. One of them was Elias Meyers and, until he was either broken or compromised, Walter refused to deal with anyone like him. Later, I learned that June rose to the challenge.

In her twisted mind, I had dropped her because I couldn't handle her. She told Brennan that she would figure out my vulnerability and break me. And once she did, I would become another sweet conquest. She called on a Saturday, quite sure that the overworked Dr. Meyers would be at his office. Actually, he was. She was eager to see Dr. Elias. She told him she wanted "to get back to work on myself." Like a putz, he agreed to take her back. The Black Widow hung up the phone, trembling in anticipation.

# THIRTEEN

Susan Decker felt a certain release after her appointment with Elias Meyers. She wrote in her diary, "It isn't that I'm sexually attracted to this little Jewish man, it's that I look into his eyes and sense his wisdom and caring. I trust him and I don't feel judged. He loaned me a little clock set to my next appointment time next Friday. So sweet, really. It's a symbol that is there to help me through the week. *If only I had found my way to him sooner! The last ten years of my life would have been different."*

Galvanized by the knowledge that she would see the doctor again soon and, as he had put it, "work this out in safety and find the life force in you", she made a decision. Later she told Elias how he had inspired her to move her life and her love ahead with breakneck speed.

Saturday nights were scheduled each week for dinner with Tim at Lautrec, the Minetta Tavern, or Olney's, all high-end bistros. They would talk about their week, which was interesting and fun, although the dates lacked intimacy or "heat." Tim was a good-looking man of accomplishment, with more than a modicum of charm. But he never flirted, squeezed her thigh or ran his hand up her leg to feel her panties. He was actually downright gentlemanly to a fault.

And she craved fireworks, something out of control that might match or challenge the feelings she experienced every Thursday night when she acted out with abandon at the club downtown. Couldn't she find a respectable man to build a life with who could also knock her off her pedestal and share her unbridled lust and sexuality?

Tim was coming to pick her up for dinner at 7:30. They planned to have drinks at The Stork Club after and then listen to jazz. Then they would return to her apartment, disrobe and have mildly pleasurable sex. Following the usual script, they would have Sunday brunch, do the *Times* crossword puzzle and say goodbye. They would talk once or twice during the week and repeat the same ritual the following week: different restaurant, same results. She loved his intellect and humor. She desired a sane life with children so she played it out each week. Yet with Dr. Meyers as an ally, she decided to change the gestalt of her relationship.

Tim knocked on her door at 7:30 and she let him in as usual. However, she was not dressed to go out. Instead, she answered the door wearing a silk robe without a sash and, underneath it, a thong and a matching pushup bra. Her hair was tousled as if she had just been done or wanted to be. Tim was taken aback.

Before he said a word she said, "Come in, sweetheart. Change of plan. I want you to strip me naked and take me. TAKE ME, Tim, and see if that makes you as happy as I want you to be."

He stood there at the threshold of her apartment seemingly aghast at her attire and at her words. The silence seemed endless, but she made no attempt to cover up, nor did he step toward her.

"What are you doing, Susie?" he asked at last.

"My body is the answer. Why are you still standing there? I'm here naked inviting you to 'take me' and you still . . . nothing? Don't you desire me? Don't you think of me as a woman who wants and needs sex . . .?

Suddenly, he crossed the threshold and ripped her clothes off. His tongue found its way down her throat and his finger into her wet vagina. He kissed her as if going off to war and then she dropped to her knees and put his hard member into her mouth. While she pleasured him he played with her nipples until they were as hard as erasers. She was overwhelmed and felt blessed. Here she was, with the man she loved, or hoped to, and he was ravaging her in ways she could only have hoped.

He entered her from behind and pulled her hair so she experienced both pain and pleasure and then she came, and more than once. Her body shuddered and she screamed—the release of a lifetime. She felt charged and in another world. She turned over and held him in her arms and looked deeply into his eyes. She was in rapture and in love. He was not a one-time stranger. She actually knew his name. "Tim . . . oh, Tim!"

Afterward, they held each other for several minutes in silence. Then she moved so she could rest on her elbow, searching for what was behind his eyes.

"Tim, I have something I must tell you, and I hope it won't change what has just happened between us."

"There's nothing that could do that," he said. "I love you, Susie. Tell me anything." He waited for her to talk, but she remained mute.

Finally, she smiled and ran her hand down his fit body. "Not now, sweetheart," she said. "We'll have plenty of time to discuss the past. For now, let's just be in the moment. Let's not talk."

He kissed her gently. She moved as close to him as two people could be and rested her head against his chest. For the time being, she had found a way to express herself with love and caring with someone who was feeling similarly fulfilled. It was a miracle.

*Not too much all at once,* she thought. Tim might bolt. And then she smiled to herself. *What would Dr. Elias say?*

# FOURTEEN

Grace and I had a great sexual relationship for a long while. She was willing and able as a partner and we often joked and shared deep conversations.

I never thought to question the fact that I seemed to have married a human chameleon. She changed her hair color, she changed haircuts, adopted different clothing. I thought she was searching for her own image and never gave it a second thought. Then she wanted to change apartments, move from Brooklyn to Manhattan. It didn't matter to me. She found a small garden apartment in a nice, upper Westside building, and when the old guy next door dropped dead of a heart attack, we broke through the thick wall and made an arched doorway two feet wide, added a bathroom, bedroom and lounge area. The boys each had a room. It was luxury. We had everything except what really mattered. "Should have, could have—but I did not wake up fast enough." I did not have the love of my life. Grace and I were emotionally parting. I denied it, minimized it. She must have also. We drifted in our own ways, away.

The phone rang, breaking my reverie. It was Rebecca.

"I'm not coming in today. Something rather exciting has come up."

I asked where she was. It was now fifteen minutes past her scheduled session. I didn't like when patients stood me up, especially on Saturdays.

"Perhaps you could have called in advance?" I suggested, somewhat peeved.

"I'm calling now," she replied petulantly.

"Rebecca, this is technically your appointment time so we can talk now or I can see you on Monday. But let's not engage in negative banter."

I had met Rebecca years ago on my first day at the clinic where I once worked, on the first day I was certified to practice. She had just been released from prison after four years of incarceration. She was only twenty-two, but looked older. Four years in an orange jump suit, and G-d knows what else, would have aged anyone.

Her story was extraordinary. She grew up in a single-story tenement surrounded by the corruption and danger of Hell's Kitchen. Her mother was a barmaid and sometimes hooker at a local dive that served rotgut liquor to angry, violent men. She had never met her father. Although she attended school intermittently, she still read at a sixth-grade level. By the time she was thirteen, she had been molested by the series of men who paraded through her mother's bedroom.

Many times Rebecca was forced to sit in the next room while her mother was having sex, as Mom didn't think it safe for Rebecca to be outside on the street alone. Rebecca would turn on their small Philco with the volume up loud to drown out the sounds, her eyes glued to the black and white screen. The mother was not unkind, just ignorant, and bewildered by the hand she had been dealt. Each passing day brought a new stranger who fucked her and threw fifty dollars on the bed. To add injury to insult, many of them felt her daughter up on the way out.

At night, Rebecca was allowed to sleep in the bedroom while her mother took the couch. One morning when she was fourteen Rebecca awoke and sensed she was alone. There was a note scribbled on lined yellow paper along with three hundred dollars in fives, tens, and at least a hundred singles. The bills were crumpled, a metaphor for the young girl's life.

Rebecca, I have gone away. I can't do any more either for myself or for you. Life is just so fucked up and it's my fault. If I had any courage I would kill us both and end everything. But I don't. I have just enough to run away and have left you all the rest. The lease on this apartment is paid for another ten days so you'll have time to figure it all out. It isn't that I don't love you. I just have to go before I lose all hope. I hope you'll be safe. Bye, Baby.

She hadn't even signed her name.

Rebecca wasn't surprised. In fact, she felt more relieved than sad. She looked around the shit hole she lived in and couldn't imagine that this was all there was in life. She was fourteen. She had a lot of years to make things better.

When she opened the dented, antiquated refrigerator she found baked beans covered in mold, and milk that was clearly sour. However, there were eight quart bottles of Ballantine Beer with the screw-off tops. Rebecca had one for breakfast. She turned on the old Philco and plopped herself on the tattered sofa. On the end table was a bottle of Jim Beam and an empty glass with her mother's lipstick on the rim. There were cartoons on TV but she couldn't say which ones. She filled the dirty glass to the rim with Mr. Beam and drank it down as if it were milk chasing an Oreo. Then she chugged half the beer. Her new life had begun. *It couldn't be worse than the last one,* she thought. Then she refilled the glass and finished the first bottle of Ballantine.

She awoke in a haze later that day, got up a bit shaky at first, steadied herself and headed to the shower. She stood under the hot, cascading water until it went cold and then brushed her teeth, put on a pair of tight blue jeans, heels and a revealing tank top. She applied lipstick and light makeup to her eyes and then brushed her pretty blonde hair until it shined. She let it hang to her shoulders somewhat unkempt on purpose.

She grabbed the three hundred dollars and walked to the corner liquor store and watched the patrons walk in and out. Quickly she found her "mark." He was a mid-forties, pot-bellied man about six feet tall. He wore a cheap suit and wrinkled white shirt with a tie that had been loosened as his workday had ended. His brow was covered with beads of sweat and, with his suit jacket thrown over his shoulder, brown perspiration stains were visible under his armpits. His thick hair was combed straight back like a film star's and Rebecca thought he might have a pleasant smile if he chose to show it.

He slowed his gait as he noticed Rebecca lingering by the door.

"What are you doing here, little girl?" he asked, with endless possibilities in his tone.

"Waiting for a man to light up my evening," she replied neatly, having heard her mother say it so many times.

"Why here in front of a booze shop?"

"I want some." Rebecca moved her hips provocatively to demonstrate.

He stared at her for a moment and then opened the door to the low-rent liquor store and took a step in.

"Wait, darling, don't you want no fun? I'll give you twenty bucks to buy me some bourbon and beer," she cooed.

"Twenty bucks don't buy a lot of fun, girlie," he said harshly.

"Yeah, but it depends on the mixer, right? You looked like a smart guy. Guess I was wrong," she added as a dig.

He closed the door to the store and walked toward Rebecca.

"Listen, kid, been a long day and I don't need no playing games. Where do you live?"

"On the corner, alone."

His eyes lit up and he again checked out her body. He liked what he saw. An unexpected way to end the week.

"OK, I'll buy you the booze, my treat, and I'll bring it to your place. Leave the door ajar."

"OK, sweetie." She imagined that she sounded much older and very tough. "But you don't get to touch me unless you bring three quarts of beer and a couple of bottles of Jim Beam. And, by the way, I'll need a fifty-dollar tip."

He nodded, smirked, and walked into the store. Within minutes he exited with a brown bag full of Rebecca's demands. He caressed her back. She pushed him away. "We got a deal. The liquor and the fifty and then the fun."

"Fine, fine, little minx. I'll meet you there in a minute. Leave the door open and I'll let myself in with your treats. You got a name?"

"Satin, like my skin," she said and turned on a dazzling smile. "See you soon, sugar."

She swayed her hips and her ego swelled. But as she walked home, her head began to pound and the too-big heels from her mother's closet fishtailed and she went over on her ankle. If this was her new life, it was certainly a lousy first day.

# FIFTEEN

When he arrived minutes later she was waiting on the couch with the door ajar. He entered the small apartment, placed the bag on the counter, found two unwashed glasses in the sink and rinsed them.

"You need a fucking maid," he said.

"I need a lot more than a maid," she replied. "You making any offers?"

"We'll see how this goes, sweetheart, then we'll talk options."

He took the bottle of whiskey out of the bag and filled each glass to the brim. Then he placed the bottle on the floor next to the couch where Rebecca was sitting.

"Drink up, doll," he commanded. "Then let's have some fun."

"My money first," she said sweetly. "That's our deal."

"Yeah, well, deals change, doll, and you're just a little whore with a hot body. I'm in charge now. You make me happy and I'll give you the dough."

She leapt off the sofa and across the room. "You liar! Nothing's going to happen here. Get out before I start screaming rape. They'll put you away for so long you'll never get it up again. You think I'm stupid? Well think again. You fuck with me we'll see who's stupid. Now what'll it be, fatso?"

He eyed her from across the small room. He was pissed but titillated. She was a fox, a young colt to be broken, and his libido (really raw anger and aggression folded into sexual sadism plus) was in high gear.

"OK, sweetheart. You're right, we had a deal. I was simply testing you . . . Kidding really. Sure I'll pay you first. Come sit next to me. We'll have another drink. You're sweet. I won't treat you bad."

He reached into his pants pocket and pulled out a wad of twenties—maybe three, four, even five hundred dollars—peeled off five of them and reached out to her.

"Here, baby," he said. "Here's a hundred bucks and you ain't done nothing 'cept drink the booze I paid for. Now let's have some fun." He smiled and it was as she had imagined, a sweet and engaging smile.

She took the hundred bucks and placed it carefully in her purse and put her purse on the countertop. She walked seductively to the couch, ready to do his bidding now that he was "a man of honor."

"What's your name, sweetie?" she asked.

"Oscar," he said. "As in Wilde." He chuckled at his joke but she had no idea what he thought was funny. He refilled the glasses and placed the empty bottle on the floor by the sofa.

"A toast! To you, Satin Doll, a pretty girl that I'm damn lucky to done met. Now drink up and let's have fun."

Once she had some booze in her, she felt a weird affection toward this stranger. Maybe it wasn't all so bad, her new life. He moved in close, kissed her on the mouth and stroked her blonde hair. She returned the kiss. He kissed her again and again and she began to get aroused. He put her hand on his hard cock and asked, "You want it, don't you girlie-girl."

"Yes," she whispered.

Then he kissed her again, but his time it was more aggressive and, before their lips parted, he grabbed her hair and pulled it so hard she had whiplash. With an easy twist of her head he could have broken her neck. Looking into her terrified eyes, he shouted, "I make the rules here, you dumb little whore. I DO!"

He began slapping her until her cheeks were numb and she thought he had broken a tooth. Her lip had split and blood dripped down her chin. Then he pulled her face to his crotch and shouted at her to unzip his pants. "Suck my cock, slut!" he screamed. "And beg me to do it."

*This is raw brutality. This is sadism. This is abuse. This is one result of neglect. This lack of a nurturing mother. This lack of a nurturing father. This is a manifestation of poverty for some.*

"May I please suck your cock?" she whimpered. As she took it from his pants and put it in her mouth, he let go of her hair and lay there while she serviced him.

"Now this is the way to behave, slut," he said with eerie sweetness.

Afterward, just as he went slack, Rebecca reached for the empty whiskey bottle next to the sofa and smashed it against his face with all the power of hatred he had just induced. He screamed in pain. Blood covered everything.

"How's that, you fuck?" she screamed at him. "Feel good, you lying scumbag?"

*This is revenge. This is pent up hatred atop of abuse. This is a lonely desperate adolescent.*

His face was bloodied with shards of glass. He whimpered in pain and asked for mercy. Instead, he got a large piece of the shattered bottled spiked into his scrotum. He screamed, but she spit in his face as he slipped into a coma.

She lit a cigarette and inhaled deeply, twice. Then she looked at what she had wrought. After going through his bloodstained pockets, which netted about six hundred bucks, she walked into the bathroom, threw up, showered, put on fresh clothes and redid her hair and makeup. She grabbed an old gym bag and filled it with some clothes and a couple of personal items, including a photo of her mother. She returned to the other room, guzzled a second bottle of rotgut and smashed the empty on the fucker's genitals.

Then she took the last bottle and soaked him and the old tattered couch. She lit another cigarette and threw the lit match on the couch. Within moments the couch was ablaze and the man who had pushed her over the edge was beginning to char.

"THAT'S FOR MY MOTHER!" she screamed.

During my first session with Rebecca, I told her that her actions were the work of a very young, incredibly terrified girl trying to avenge her mother. She shrugged. The truth is, her murderous deed showed an enormous love, albeit an unrequited one, for her lost parent. It was, in a twisted way, an honor killing.

Once she was sure that the man called Oscar was dead, she opened the door to the apartment and walked out into the lovely spring evening. She willed her insane trembling to stop; willed herself to walk slowly toward the corner to catch a cab to the bus station. The house was in full blaze behind her and there were sirens in the distance.

Rebecca bought a ticket to the next bus leaving town. Coach #721 headed for Boston. She paid her $11.50 fare, bought a NY Yankees baseball cap, a pair of large sunglasses and a few movie magazines. She sat alone in the back of the bus and munched a Snickers bar, washing it down with the beer she had brought with her.

She slept on and off on during the four-hour ride. She didn't spend a moment thinking about what she had just done but, rather, about what she was going to do. She was uneducated and had no marketable job skills. But she was fearless and she was a looker. She could make a man's pulse race and, for the immediate future, that would do. Luckily, she looked older than she was and had almost a thousand dollars. She would take her time figuring out her next step. With her looks and instincts, she intended to make her money in fancy hotel rooms drinking expensive champagne.

The best laid plans.

She arrived in Boston after 10 p.m. and asked her cabbie to suggest a modest hotel. After she had checked in at The Parker House, the bellman showed her to her room and went on and on about the history of the establishment. She didn't hear a word and he left disappointed that she hadn't been taken by his charm, nor had she tipped him. She took a hot shower, ordered room service and lay undressed until the food arrived. When she answered the door naked, the waiter nearly fainted, alternating between red-faced stuttering and all-out gawking as he laid out the food.

Finally, she sat crossed-legged on the bed and ate some of the best food she had ever tasted, accompanied by a fine wine, since no one had thought to check her ID. She flipped on the color TV and watched some movie with a tall actor by the name of Rock Hudson and some blonde babe named Doris Day. She drank, she ate, she felt the soft spring breeze through the window caress her skin while she watched Doris and Rock fall in love. She hadn't completely forgotten that hours earlier she had burned a man to death but, as each moment passed, it seemed like a bad dream from which she had finally awakened.

# SIXTEEN

"Doctor? Dr. Meyers? Are you still there?" Rebecca asked with some degree of panic.

I had been half-listening to her while taking stock of my own mental health and her toll on it. I liked to tell myself that when I closed the office door, I left the dysfunctional, the lonely and lost behind. That when I turned off the lights to go to sleep, their stories would evaporate in the darkness. Yes, that was the way it was supposed to work. But the numerous shrinks whom I had hired from time to time over the years to analyze me had made little progress. As it turned out, I was no less tortured than my patients.

My priorities had gone askew. For instance, I seldom saw my sons, never gave them a thought. Of course, I provided for them and made perfunctory small talk with them on mundane subjects, but never saw them play a game on their school team, never helped with a homework assignment anymore or took them to a ballgame. My work was a wall that had increasingly risen around me on all sides, a wall of narcissism that overshadowed all else.

"DR. MEYERS!" Rebecca shouted.

"Yes, Rebecca. I'm still here."

"I thought you hung up." She sensed that I had checked out. She was astute, could smell insincerity. I had to stay on my toes.

"I wouldn't do such a thing."

"I suppose I should trust that by now. Can I tell you my news?"

"As I've said, this is your time. But I don't like phone sessions, so just this once."

There was a pause. In that moment I wondered why she often made me so weary. Perhaps it was because she had come so far yet remained so fragile and damaged. Finally, she jumped in with the enthusiasm of a cheerleader. "Doctor, Danny had a wonderful idea and because of his influence we can get it done today and begin making money tomorrow!"

"Influence?"

"You know, how he makes things happen by paying cash. People move faster. He gets to the front of the line. It's really quite wonderful," she said.

"Rebecca, take a moment to reflect. You're involved with this married man in ways I don't know about but I'm concerned that they will bring you trouble . . ."

"You're so g-ddamned negative, Elias. Such a downer. Why can't you be happy for me? Danny is so sweet and he's helping me!"

"Forgive me, but I *am not* a 'downer,' Rebecca. My job is to help you find the life you want. What do you really know of Danny? Where does he get all that cash anyway?"

"What difference does that make?" She sounded like a hurt fifteen-year-old.

"I don't want you to make choices that set you back to the dark days when you were like an abused dog who, by the grace of G-d and your will, we rescued from the kill shelter!"

"Oh stop it!" she shouted. "That was years ago. That's no longer me."

She was right. I was wrong to bring up ancient history. She had made a lot of progress with me. Was I feeling jealous that this Danny was somehow replacing me as her savior? I struggled to find the calm, non-judgmental tone I normally used.

"You're absolutely right, Rebecca, you're no longer that person. Now, tell me what's so important that you're missing your session?"

"Well, Danny bought a condo in midtown at a great price because he paid cash. His idea is to dress the entire bedroom in mirrors so when my clients come to meet their girls it's a 'show.' He says it's better value for the dollar and it will accelerate our revenue goals. Then I can get out of the biz and do what you and I want me to do! See? It's a wonderful opportunity. But we both have to be here today to oversee the installation."

Again Rebecca was about to step in quicksand. Her "Danny Boy" was no savior. In fact, he was no different than the men who had hurt Rebecca when she was younger, left her to die, led her to prison addicted to heroin. Her courage had gotten her through it. But this Mr. Schwartzberg was the devil. He was the new needle in Rebecca's arm and if she stayed with him she would crash and burn. And with hope just around the corner! It was difficult to stay calm.

"Rebecca, you've spent a lifetime escaping your past and, as Shakespeare said, 'Past is prologue.' What you have now is a present and you have to make the healthy choice here."

"I don't need your quotes from famous people, Doctor. Who made you the judge and jury of my life anyway?"

"You did. The state did when they released you from prison," I replied. "You're in a dangerous place, Rebecca. I have no intention of discussing this further on a telephone call. It's your life and I share my disapproval only out of concern for your well-being." (What did I really know?)

I was becoming increasingly detached to protect my own feelings. (My transference worry about being erotic mistakingly is better at affection and tenderness—life giving . . .)

"You have another session on Monday. Please show up on time and ask Danny to join us some fifteen minutes later. Understood? Your judgment is still that of a damaged little girl looking for love. You need to get yourself here Monday!"

"You don't sound very friendly," she said in a voice both flirtatious and petulant. (She is right. She is worried. She does not want to lose parental care, even if she has to flirt to keep that nurturance.)

"I am friendly but I'm not your friend. I'm your doctor. Are you committed to keeping your appointment on Monday? Yes or no, Rebecca?" (I am defensive and plum wrong.)

There was a long silence; I could hear her angry, disoriented breathing.

"Fine," she said, when she really meant "fuck you." She understood the doctor-patient relationship but wished it were more. She wished that I could be her father . . . and her husband. (And G-d knows what I thought and felt at that moment.)

Then the line went dead.

# SEVENTEEN

After she hung up, I grabbed her file and back to Rebecca's past I went, trying to pick up the threads of our work together. She had come so far! Now she seemed to be taking a detour that would lead her back to square one.

The teenager who had checked into the Porter House hoping for a life of room service and rich men had hit a great many potholes. The locale was indeed elegant and the men wealthy and well dressed, but no one cared for her or loved her. So she figured she was only worthy on her back or knees. She learned quickly that wealth did not equal manners or respect and that having sex with men who paid her was a dead end. She drank too much to get though ugly nights being fucked by strangers who had no regard for her. The money didn't gain her anything except self-loathing.

She turned sixteen but looked like a hardened adult, beautiful, robotic and without humanity. The Parker House asked her to leave a few months into her stay as they became aware of her calling. She left quietly. To some degree, she felt fortunate. Since no one had traced her in all this time, it seemed that she had gotten away with murder—wise to move on.

She moved to a lesser hotel nearby where they asked fewer questions. The Beacon Hotel was once a prize place to stay but now it bordered on the "Combat Zone," Boston's seedy neighborhood of street walkers, pimps, drug dealers and mobile johns who drove by in expensive cars looking for a blow job for fifty dollars or a tryst on a side street in the back seat of a "Caddy." Just blocks away were the Boston Commons, with its magnificent history, and Beacon Hill, where the Meyers resided and the Ritz towered over Back Bay.

She went for a driver's license and discovered that she had no social security number or birth certificate. So she bought an identity with falsified documents that allowed her to get an ID and driver's license, which she never actually used to drive. She was clever, but with each passing moment she became more tired and depressed. With each passing month she moved closer to despair and lost the will to fight her descent.

By eighteen she was living on the streets, sleeping in alcoves of buildings and trading sex with corrupt cops so they wouldn't lock her up. She was a street whore, fucking for twenty bucks or less. Anything that afforded her enough smack to get her high for a while and delay the inevitable dance with the devil.

She no longer had plans or hopes or dreams. She was a wild animal with no sense of morality or what dangers she attracted. Despite her fall from grace she found ways to clean up nicely in public rest rooms or the bathroom of some hotel lobby. On rare occasions, when a john would invite her to his hotel room, she could groom herself and even feel pretty again.

On the night when a dark Mercedes sedan slowed on her corner, she no longer knew her birthday, had friends or a shred of hope.

"Hey, honey," a drunken voice shouted, "you're pretty hot and sexy to be out alone. Why not come party with us, sweetheart? Have a few drinks, do a few lines and HAVE A GOOD TIME!"

The car stopped and the four hammered and horny young men inside gawked at her. Rebecca knew the type. She knew she retained true sexual allure and that sexual allure gave her a small modicum of power.

"I don't do frat boys. And you're all drunk and whacked to boot. I doubt any of you could find your dick let alone get it hard. You're probably all faggots."

"Fuck you, bitch," one of them sneered. "You're a slut afraid to be with real men. You're a twenty-dollar blow job for any joker who drives by!"

Another one of them jumped out. He was tall and fit with dark, wavy hair and clear green eyes. He was calm and flirty, winning and winsome.

"I'm sorry for my friends," he said. "They can get rude sometimes, but down deep they're good guys . . . my buddies, you know. We all go to Boston College and, well, we were looking for some out-of-the-box fun tonight. But their behavior is really . . . well, inappropriate and I'm sorry."

He took her hand in his and walked with her down the block as if they were a couple. Rebecca felt something she had never felt before. Connection?

"What's your name?"

"Rebecca."

"I apologize for all of us, Rebecca," he said. "I'm Dean and I want to give you this money as a gesture of my contrition. You're sweet."

"Contrition" was a word Rebecca didn't know but she felt warmth from Dean and she needed the money.

"Thank you, sweetheart. If your friends are as nice as you we could still play. I like you, Dean."

He looked at her for a long time as if he were struggling with a decision. "Listen, babe, my pals are lit and they're all going to want to do you, maybe at the same time. Is that what you really want? Let me just give you another hundred and go home without getting it on with them."

"Why? You don't think I haven't done that stuff before?"

"Maybe you have, but I like you and I don't want it to get weird for you when my buddies are treating you like a whore."

"I am a whore, Dean. They don't have girls like me at Boston College and that's why you boys are out on the prowl. Not everyone gets to go to Boston College, Dean. Some of us are dealt bad hands and to bet is to lose. So we fold and live day to day."

"And what happens tomorrow?" he asked.

"Same shit. Different faces, no names. It doesn't matter because there's no way out. But that doesn't mean I don't matter. I'm still a person. My heart beats just like yours but I'm invisible while you and your buddies run the world."

"Go home, Rebecca." His voice expressed what seemed like shame. "Here's a hundred bucks." He began to walk back toward the car.

In all the years I have worked with Rebecca, despite all the professionalism and objectivity I can muster, I still cringe at what happened next.

"I'll go with you all, if *you* want me," she called after him.

He stopped and turned slowly. "You sure, babe?" he asked. "It might get pretty nasty."

"Listen, honey, boys from Boston College don't come close to my definition of nasty. You want me or not?"

"How much, Rebecca?" He couldn't disguise his eagerness.

"Fifteen hundred and room service. Cash up front."

"Deal!" he said quickly. "We have a suite at the Copley. Room 807. Here's twenty. Grab a cab. We'll be waiting for you."

"See you there, Dean. Be sweet to me. It doesn't happen often."

She leaned into him and kissed his lips softly, as if he were her boyfriend. He kissed her back. His lips were baby soft.

"All sweet, babe, I promise."

## EIGHTEEN

The lobby of The Copley Plaza was opulent beyond imagination. The bright red rugs were plush and the polished elevator doors gleamed like giant mirrors. The privileged clientele drank their martinis in the old oak bar off the lobby and spoke in hushed tones. Rebecca walked briskly through this strange world hoping no one would stop her and ask what someone like her was doing in The Copley. She had an answer ready but it wasn't necessary. Nobody noticed as she stepped into the elevator and pressed eight.

She was home free and ready for a lucrative sex romp with some young frat boys, followed by expensive food and wine. And who knew what else? Maybe Dean would ask her out on a real date. (Her real wish, rather healthy, however unreal— poor judgment confused, yearning.) Before she knocked on room 807 she snorted a dollop of smack for courage.

Dean opened the door wearing boxer shorts and nothing else. He took her hand and led her into the suite and introduced his buddies as Sam, Bob and Jake. Their names didn't matter. They were all partially naked, lounging on the expensive furniture, wired on coke. There was enough remaining on the coffee table for a battalion of horny boys.

"Come in, babe," said Dean. "I already ordered room service and it's on the way. Bubbly and caviar and a bunch of á la carte. Why don't you go freshen up? There's a robe in the bathroom you can change into and then we can all get acquainted."

She looked around the expensive room. These boys were so smart, so rich, having such fun. Yet she sensed something ominous. Something was off, simply not right. She hesitated a moment. Had she listened to the danger siren from her limbic system she would have turned and fled that room instantly.

"Move it, sweetie!" Dean's jocular tone reassured her and she did as she was told.

The bathroom was lush and the sink surrounded by lotions with delicious scents; promises of anti-aging and stress reduction. She took off her clothes and looked at her body in the three-way mirror. It was fabulous. G-d had blessed her with a perfect, sexy, smooth body. Her belly was flat and her legs long and soft and toned. Her ass was pear-shaped and her breasts stood at attention. She took some lube from her handbag and rubbed it on her vagina and up her ass. She then put on the hotel's robe, made from the softest terry cloth on earth, tied the sash and entered the living room ready for work.

The energy in the room was even more manic than when she had left to change just moments ago. Dean and his friends were now totally naked. Although plenty of coke remained on the glass coffee table, clearly a lot had disappeared up those noses in the meantime.

Room service had arrived on a big cart, all dressed in white tablecloths and folded napkins. There was a panoply of goodies to eat and half a dozen bottles of high-end Champagne.

One of the guys gave her a glass to drink and she sipped it. This was not what he wanted.

"Chug it, sweetie," he challenged, downing his own. And she did. Then she was handed another and another and one more, all gone in minutes. There was laughter all around and she was laughing too.

"Now get really happy. You gotta play catch up!" Another of the boys grabbed her roughly by the hair and put her face in the pile of coke. She had no choice but to snort like a pig in order to breathe—took in what might have been the equivalent of six or eight lines in seconds. Finally, he stepped back and let her up. Rebecca was so high the room moved like a kaleidoscope and her face was covered with the cocaine.

"Oooooh," one of the boys snapped. "You look like a fucking ghoul!"

She struggled to speak. "Yeah, I must look pretty strange. I'll go wash it off . . ."

"No you don't, honey," one of them said as he grabbed her arm and spun her around. It was Dean! He held a bottle of champagne, shook it vigorously and then sprayed it all over her face and washed away the white powder.

Then the largest in the group stripped off the robe and threw her onto the plush blue couch. During the split second she was airborne she saw the Boston skyline glimmering outside the window. It looked like Oz, the city where dreams come true.

Two of the boys spread her legs till she was afraid they might snap. Another sprayed her genitals with champagne. They cackled like animals as Dean mounted her in one painful thrust. She cried out in pain, and he slapped her across the face and began pumping her as if she were a rag doll. Within seconds he pulled out and sprayed his cum all over her breasts and chin. The other three followed the same routine as if they had practiced. When they were all finished Dean told her to lick it off and clean up as the fun was just starting.

(This is a repeat of her poor judgement, her innocence, her greed, and beneath it all a buried healthy desire, not to be attained in her mental state.)

They let her lie on the expensive sofa and whispered among themselves about what to do with her next. Soon Dean came over, sat next to her and insisted she drink some more. She slurred a "no" so he pulled her hair back and poured it down her throat until she was drowning. This was no sex romp. These men were evil, and her life hung in peril. (Repeated again and again.) Perhaps this was the night when it would all end, she thought. Maybe that was a good thing. (Shame, desperate, great pain, emotional and physical—suicide in the making.)

She staggered to her feet as if underwater. Everything was blurred and in slow motion. Nevertheless, she sensed they were planning to amp up their kicks. Dean had opened a bottle of bourbon and they passed it around, each taking a slug and following with a line of coke. The largest guy held handcuffs. The kid with blonde shaggy hair had taken off his belt and snapped it playfully towards her.

Somehow she found a way to hold her balance. It took all her strength, but she remained standing despite her nausea and fear. She took several deep breaths and her head cleared a little.

"Hey, honey, what's up? Where do you think you're going? Your boys here were just making plans for some more fun. That's what you came for right, sweetheart?"

Rebecca's base instincts kicked in. "Boys! My naughty boys," she said in a throaty, suggestive voice. "You think for one second that I'm done with you? I need those cocks. I'm a bad girl. I want to eat your cum and beg for more . . ."

"Whooo!" they screamed in unison. It was like Christmas morning. She used the opportunity to escape.

"I'm going to use the rest room, make myself sweeter than ever. Just give me a few moments to freshen up," she said, adding a wink as she massaged their cum all over her breasts. "Just keep those dicks hard till I get back."

Somehow she found her way to the bathroom and locked herself inside. There in front of her a stranger stared back, eyes glazed, face deathly white. She turned on the shower, knelt by the toilet and stuck her finger down her throat. Loud rock music blared in the living room along with the crazy laughter of jackals. Her heart beat with the escalation of the drugs and the mortal fear of their pack mentality. There was a loud pounding on the door and the handle jiggled.

"Hey, why'd you lock this door?"

"Just getting pretty for you all. Won't be more than a few seconds," she replied sweetly.

She pulled on her jeans and tank top and stepped into her heels. She grabbed her bag and took out the small can of mace she carried with her and the small .25 Beretta she had only fired once in the past years. She wanted to die but not at their hands. (Good judgement at the moment, strong will, still suicidal.)

She drank a large glass of water and then another to quell her nerves. By now there was angry pounding on the door. She slung her bag over her shoulder and opened the door with the gun in one hand and the mace in the other. The big guy was standing directly in front of her. When he saw she was dressed, anger creased his face.

"What the fuck are you doing?" He raised a hand. She pointed the mace at his face and sprayed him. He screamed out in pain and grabbed his eyes, and then flailed his arms in an attempt to grab her. He couldn't see shit.

It took the others a moment to register what was happening.

"You cunt!" Dean shouted. He took a step toward her and she pointed the gun at his crotch.

"You ain't doing nothing." Her voice was razor sharp. "You move and I'll shoot your cock off and then I'll shoot your fucking friends, your BUDDIES! You cocksuckers! I'm leaving. Now out of my way!"

The room was without air. The big guy was whimpering, his hands covering his eyes. Dean and his pals were stunned. High and absolutely stunned.

"I said out of my way," Rebecca shouted. "Now!"

No one moved.

A smirk crossed Dean's face and he laughed at her, spreading his arms wide as if welcoming danger.

"Go ahead, shoot me you bitch." He laughed mockingly.

So she shot him.

The bullet grazed his thigh and he collapsed to the floor

"Fuck!" he shouted. "You motherfucker."

The other two boys remained by the table, blocking her path. Shocked and afraid.

"Move, you piss ants," Rebecca said in a reasoned voice. "I said MOVE!"

Suddenly she was hit in the small of her back by the big guy she had blinded with mace. He couldn't see straight but was strong and, even off balance and in pain, he was able to knock her to the floor. Like a blindsided quarterback, she went down hard. Her head hit the polished wood and the gun skittered away. The "mace guy" grabbed her hair, pulled her to her feet and yanked her head back so hard she thought he'd break her neck. Screaming curses, he punched her in the stomach and knocked the air out of her. He hit her again just above her ear. The side of her head began to bleed. He let go and she fell to the floor, barely conscious. (I repeat, she again and again does not execute her thoughts for leaving danger behind. Her conflicting emotions, her history of neglect and abuse take over and she again loses. She needs to be institutionalized, treated, and then followed by outpatient treatment with a professional who could endure the ups and downs of long-term treatment. Short-term work will not suffice.)

Dean had found his way to the sofa and ordered one of his cronies to get a towel to wrap his leg. The mace guy had disappeared into the bathroom and she heard water running. She imagined he was washing his eyes before returning to beat her some more.

"Get dressed. Pack up. We're out of here," Dean commanded.

The blonde kid walked over and kicked her in the ribs three or four or five times. She couldn't tell. Breathing was beyond painful. He ripped off her top and slapped her breasts so they were red as if sunburnt. He then grabbed her face and shook her head.

"Stay with us, bitch. I want you to feel what's coming. Give you something to remember us by." He pulled down her jeans. The mace guy stood over the bed, as did Dean who was held up by the third pal. They turned up the music and took turns beating her with the belt as she squirmed helplessly beneath them. It was endless.

Dean rummaged through her handbag, pocketed her money and found four little envelopes filled with smack. Two of them he kept. The other two he placed on the floor near her gun. He found her lipstick and in big red letters wrote the word "whore" on her back.

"Now let's say goodbye to our nice little friend." He staggered backwards, took a last look at the battered and abused young woman and smirked.

Through swollen eyes, she watched as Dean limped to the door, leaning on his cronies. "Turn off the lights and the music," he ordered. Then he closed the door on the obscenity. The maid later testified that the "do not disturb" sign on the knob kept her from opening the room until she heard moaning as she was going off shift the following night.

Apparently, the three amigos slipped down the stairs to the darkened bar and out the side entrance. Months later, in exchange for a lighter sentence, one of them ratted Dean out and told police that Dean did a snort of amyl nitrate to shake the pain of his gunshot wound, then they walked half a block to Copley Square, hailed a cab and told the driver to take them to a parking lot adjacent to the Boston Garden. They didn't care about the Mercedes. It wasn't theirs; they had stolen it earlier that evening and checked in at the hotel with false ID.

They paid the cabby and walked slowly to their car, a beat up Ford Bronco with Ohio plates. They figured they'd be home by early morning and make it to the steel mill with time to spare. Dean would call in sick and lie low for a day. Their jobs were dead end so Dean created these adventures so they could "blow off steam", four of them, so far, in four different cities.

Their next outing was to be two months later. The next weeks were filled with talk of what they had done, what they were planning on doing. They were "just being boys."

Clearly, they had surrendered to pack mentality with Dean as the Alpha. To themselves, they had become invincible. There was no way anyone could possibly connect the events in Room 807 with them, and most likely "the whore would die anyway."

But the cops got lucky. Dean had dropped his wallet on the floor of the cab and their incoherent boasting had raised the cabbie's suspicions. When he turned it in, he saved the next Rebecca from a terrible fate.

Rebecca drifted in and out of consciousness. She was vaguely aware of knocks on the door from housekeeping but she didn't have the strength to respond. The phone rang once, twice, several times. She felt as if she were going to die and wished it would happen soon.

Some twenty hours after the boys had "checked out," she was discovered by the maid and taken to Boston General Hospital. Three days later the police grilled her, despite the fact she was heavily medicated. They treated her like a tramp. Except one of them, a well-dressed detective in his late twenties with prematurely gray, salt-and-pepper hair, wearing a dark suit and blue tie. He said not a word but listened intently with a look of knowing on his face. When the questioning was complete, he walked to her bedside, squeezed her hand gently and whispered, "You've hit rock bottom, young lady. There's no place for you to go except up. I'll pray for you."

She heard him through the haze, the voice of an angel.

Rebecca was indicted by the Boston DA for prostitution, possession of narcotics with intent to sell, and carrying an unlicensed firearm. Her previous arrests were piled on. The public defender assigned to her was a young woman who seemed bored and frustrated that all her fancy law-school education had led her to this lowlife client. Knowing she would probably lose, she insisted Rebecca plead down. So Rebecca was sentenced to eight years in the Manituck Women's Prison, released four years later for good behavior on condition that she meet extensively with a therapist. Two days after her release she walked into my life. No one ever connected Rebecca to her murdering her first client.

# NINETEEN

I remember reading Rebecca's case just before we met for her first session and was sickened by the description. The men were low-life animals who had defiled her and left her to die. *Pure cruelty*, I thought. How could people behave in such a way? The right side of the brain . . . was it all in there at birth? Could I hope to fend off the demons that must haunt this poor victim?

I wasn't sure I had the stomach. Why not leave this difficult specialty of really abused and disturbed people and go into general counseling? I'd still make good money for shorter hours and less trauma. Yet Rebecca was outside in the waiting room and I knew I was one of a handful of doctors with the talent, patience, and own "insanity" to get her past the horror. Years and years later, I was still trying. I could only pray that she would keep her appointment on Monday so I could steer her away from the threat of her beloved Danny Boy. (I am blinded. He was good for her—he met nurturing needs, economic security, and he indeed "loved" her.)

One of my clocks went off. Ethan Clark and his wife would arrive soon. I picked up a little picture of Grace that still sat among the clocks. After all the years, I couldn't bear to get rid of it. She was standing by an old barn on the property we used to own in Cherry Valley, our little blue clapboard house in the distance. She was wearing a straw sun hat, her head tilted, hands on hips. I think she was pregnant with Spencer.

We loved finding old, beat-up furniture. I would strip the surfaces and sand them smooth. Grace was great at refinishing and polishing. Working with my hands, I would totally lose myself, my overly analytical mind would finally shut down. It was just the two of us, side by side. But, looking back, I remember the furniture we worked on together, not our conversations, not the plans we made or feelings we shared. Despite our shared interests and mutual respect, we were already growing apart in tastes, values, and views of the world. Intimacy was fading fast. Oddly enough, I did remember the patients I was treating at the time, the complexity of each case.

Maybe all the nights I had listened to my parents discuss the horrors of Hitler's vast evil had influenced my decision to zoom in on one life at a time. I couldn't save an overwhelming world of souls, but I could save a few. I placed Grace's picture carefully back in its little forest of clocks and forced myself to leave my musings on the past. Looking toward the future was the only way to heal.

I made some coffee and sipped slowly, waiting for the eccentric Ethan Clark to arrive with his wife. I often pondered the fact that people who are physically scarred get a sympathetic pass from society, as their woes are easy to see and understand. Mental illness is hidden to the naked eye, a stigma implying weakness or lack of courage that is suspect, unacceptable to society.

There was a hard, purposeful knock on the office door at 2 p.m. on the dot. Ethan Clark was prompt if nothing else. I opened the door and Clark stood there beaming, as if he had just doubled down on a pair of aces and had two kings winking back at him. He was dressed as if his next stop was the roof garden at the Peninsula or the Kentucky Derby. His shoes were shined and he wore a turquoise seersucker suit with a white cotton button down and cobalt tie. He was tan and calm and cool. Behind him stood not one, but five women.

Four of them were starlet pretty, showing their firm, tight figures in revealing pastel spring dresses. They were manicured and their hair was coifed, their makeup subtle and alluring. They walked in uninvited while the fifth woman lingered behind. She was plain but sweetly attractive, slightly chubby with rosy cheeks and glossy, auburn hair. She was clean-scrubbed and her cotton suit was taupe and shapeless.

Ethan took her hand and said sweetly, "Come in, honey. The doctor's waiting." It was easy to figure out who was who in this line up.

How could one man manage five women? How did Evan cope with their emotions, their varying needs? Where did he find the energy! Well, I was about to find out.

# TWENTY

My office had not been designed for large group sessions but I eventually choreographed the bodies into a tolerable seating arrangement. The soft-shouldered group of "Daisy Mays" settled in as one on the couch while Ethan took the club chair. His "plain Jane" sat off to the side in a smaller chair I pulled from my desk. Ethan reached out and took hold of her hand.

I surveyed the scene, somewhat amused. I had requested a meeting with the wife and her busy husband. Instead I was confronted with his entire harem as if his home were somewhere in Utah. And then I realized one was missing. He had come this far in revealing his secret life. Where was the stray?

"So, Doctor, I brought my wife, Holly, as requested." He gestured to her as if she were an urn in a pottery shop. Holly nodded, confirming her identity. "And then I thought, you know, in order to speed up the process of fixing me, I'd bring the whole group." Ethan beamed proudly.

Silence. The women on the couch shifted slightly.

"So, Doc, what do we do? How do we fix me?"

"Mr. Clark," I began.

"Ethan. Call me Ethan," he interjected.

"I can't fix you. You're not a flat tire or a broken lamp. You're a complex, successful man who needs serious attention and I need more information in order to even begin to help you."

110

His raised his eyebrows. "What kind of information! What do you need? Holly, tell him I'm a good husband and all that stuff."

His wife smiled meekly. "My husband is a good husband." She parroted him even down to the intonation.

"You see. What did I tell you?"

I couldn't remember nor, frankly, was I interested in the names of the pastel quartet so I refer to them by the colors they wore.

Canary Yellow and Hot Pink chimed in. "Yes that's so true. ET is a wonderful man!" "And also a terrific father and—" "—a great lover—" "—the envy of any girl!" Their accolades overlapped so it was hard to tell who felt what. It also seemed Mr. Clark was an alien, as his nickname was ET. He was playing the role just fine.

"Ethan, why isn't your other girlfriend here today?"

He frowned darkly.

"She said she had plans today and couldn't change them because it was Saturday. I urged her to reconsider and even offered an additional stipend but she passed."

"Passed? And how did that make you feel?"

"Well, pissed off! I mean, really pissed off. After all I done for her, she couldn't make it here to help fix me."

"Are you surprised the woman requested more money to help you? Are these relationships based on concern or on the bottom line?" I asked.

The girl in the sea-foam sundress and lavender lips entered the fray. "When ET called and told me she betrayed him, I was so upset. I told him I'd call some girlfriends and he wouldn't have to miss a beat. We can replace that bitch in no time." She smiled proudly.

"Is that a good thing?" I asked. Her look became confused.

Despite the bravado with which Clark had arrived, he was becoming anxious. He stood and paced as he had during our meeting yesterday afternoon.

"Mrs. Clark," I said, "how did your husband get you to come today to meet me?"

"He said he was in trouble and that you could help him if I met you. So I came."

"Did he say what kind of trouble?"

She offered a small chuckle as if the question was silly.

"Why would that matter? If Nee-Nee is in danger I wouldn't ask questions. I would just show up and do what he asked of me."

"Nee-Nee?"

"Oh, Ethan's nickname."

Nee-Nee and his alter ego, ET, beamed at her.

"What if your husband did something immoral, stole from someone or acted outside the law. Would you still support him without reservation?"

"That would never happen," she said, suddenly assertive.

Sea Foam spoke up with irritation. "Why are you asking ET's wife all these questions?"

"Do you not know Mr. Clark's wife's name?"

Miss Sea Foam obviously had no idea, which embarrassed her not at all. "I don't date her, I date her husband."

"Do you know his children's names?"

"Why should I? I don't date them either. I date ET and I *know* his name."

"Yes, you do. Of course." It was time to push farther. "Do you know what kind of work he does?"

Sea Foam jumped to her feet and turned to face Ethan. "What the fuck is this, Ethan? Some quiz show? Some test? Maybe I should have studied up on this shit, huh? Well, I don't like being here and I don't like this little Jew doctor either . . ."

She paused a moment, expecting him to step in and protect her from the "little Jew doctor." Instead he sat there with an expression of discovery on his face.

"You have nothing to say to me, ET?" She put her hands on her hips.

He stared at her, and then at me.

"Well then fuck you, cockroach!" she shouted at him. "All cozy with your kyke bastard!" Her face was flushed and her eyes filled with fury. Suddenly, I felt as though I were watching a movie starring the most foul-mouthed, albeit the most magnificent, creature I had ever seen. She stormed to the door and turned. Mrs. Clark stood up.

"Guys like you, Ethan, are dick-less wonders. You get girls like me because of your money and your charisma. Well, that seems to have dried up this morning so—"

Before she could say another word Mrs. Clark took a step toward her and cracked her across the face.

"Get out," she said to the shocked beauty. "And stay away from my husband, you little slut. Cockroach? Ha! You're the cockroach and, by the way, that green dress makes your skin look sallow."

She shoved her, catapulting the woman backwards into the hallway, teetering wildly on her four-inch heels.

Once the door slammed Holly became calm. "Sorry, Doctor, let's continue. Sometimes these women really get me mad . . . just so mad."

Ethan sat, shocked. Holly resumed her seat next to him, wiping her hands as though she had just thrown out the garbage.

"So, girls," Ethan began sheepishly, turning toward the remaining three. "Do any or all of you feel the way Rosie does . . . did?"

The three of them looked toward me as if I were going to offer advice.

Of course I said nothing.

"Well." Canary Yellow cleared her throat. "Well, first let me say, I like Jews. In fact, I love Matzo Ball soup so all that mean stuff is, well, terrible. In fact, I once dated a Jew. So there."

"I'm a Jew," Ethan said.

"Oh?" said Canary Yellow. "I never knew. No matter. Like I said, I like Jews. Wouldn't marry one but I like them." She stood to go. "But I've always wanted to ask, what is it with those beanies?"

Hot Pink stood up quickly and grabbed her things.

"Jewish? Ethan, you never told me? How could I explain it to my friends? I can't see you anymore. Sorry." She kissed him on the cheek and headed for the door. And then, before she left, she turned to me. "I'm not a terrible person, Doc. I mean, I hated that whole Holocaust thing, all you poor Jews. I mean the beanies are in bad taste, but really!"

They left together in solidarity.

Beanies caused the Holocaust? Who knew? Where did Ethan find these girls and, more importantly, why?

And, just as in an Agatha Christie mystery, "then there was one."

Sky Blue looked very much like the deposed Sea Foam. They were twins, as a matter of fact. Right now, she looked very concerned, and I couldn't wait for what she was about to say except that, for the first time in all my years of practicing, I was about to break into hysterical laughter. Beanies and a bevy of beauties bolting one by one!

I stalled by offering coffee. Thank G-d Mrs. Clark did want some. Bless her heart for giving me the chance to turn my back with my face contorted and shoulders shaking. Thank G-d I was able to get myself under control. That was a good thing, because the best was yet to come.

"ET, me and my sister are both going to move on. It just doesn't seem right anymore. I mean, all us girls and you being married and all and to such a nice girl. Although if I were you, Mrs. Clark, honey, I'd lose ten maybe fifteen pounds."

I faked a coughing fit. Ethan pounded my back sympathetically and I pulled myself together again. He took the cup and passed it to his wife.

Sky Blue hardly missed a beat. "ET, you're a nice fellow, handsome and generous, and when we had sex it was, no offence, just OK. I mean, you're so neurotic, talking about that guy, Frankie. It seemed I was spending more time in bed with him than you. And then, you have kids. So I just realized there's no future in this for me or my sister."

I had to ask, just had to know. "Miss, were you with Ethan knowing there were so many others?"

"You know, Doctor, people think pretty women are dumb, but not all of us are. It's a gift to be pretty. Who asks to be ugly? So we all use our gifts, right? G-d gave you smarts and you became a doctor. A Jewish one, but nevertheless." (Yet I knew from the age of ten I wanted to help the world, although I had no unique visions.) "Mickey Mantle was given the gift to be a great baseball player and he aced it—made a lot of money. No one judged him. In fact, they cheered him.

"Why Ethan? He's handsome, sweet like a puppy, buys great gifts and wants nothing more than for me to listen to his problems. I don't worry about a date on Wednesday and we always eat at nice places."

"What about the immorality of it all?" I asked. "His marriage?"

"Ask her." She nodded toward his wife. "It's been fun Ethan. Nice meeting you, Mrs. Clark." And she left.

Before any of us could react, the door reopened. "Just for the record I wanted to say two things. One, when he's a bit drunk, ET gives great head. Two, there was no Holo-caust. The whole thing was made up so there could be lots of movies based on it all. I'm an actress so I've read about this stuff. See you at the pictures. Bye now."

And then there were none . . . just Ethan, his wife and the Jew whose parents had escaped the Holocaust . . . if it ever actually happened.

# TWENTY-ONE

"Are you OK, honey?" Holly asked. She sat on the club chair opposite him, but the distance seemed to have grown.

"How should I be?"

"Happy. Relieved."

"Relieved to be abandoned?"

"I'm still here, sitting across from you. Doesn't that count for anything?" For the first time there was edge in her tone.

He didn't seem to hear her. "What am I going to do now? That fucking Frankie! This is all his fault!" he cried out to no one in particular. (He needs work. She is many things, one of which is a moral masochistic character—look that up if you so wish—plus other things I need not say.)

She stood up and smacked him on the side of the head. (*Great, good for you,* I thought.) He looked up at her, stunned. He looked at me. I shrugged.

"First, you need to fire Frankie. He works for *you*. You're the one who started the company from nothing and built it into a huge success. Remember selling stuff out of your car? Well, start over. Sell the house, my wedding ring, the cars, and within months you'll be back on top."

He stared at his shiny shoes. I said nothing.

She was gathering steam. "Secondly, spend more time with the boys. They'll be gone faster than you think. Be a man! Teach them how to play catch, go to a ballgame; help them with homework." That certainly resonated with me.

"You don't think I'm a man?" he asked, hurt and confused.

Of all that she had just said, all he heard was, "Be a man!"

It was unfolding beautifully.

"You have a man inside you somewhere, but you aren't letting him grow up. This doctor may be able to help you, but you have to try to fix your own damn self. And while you're at it, why not have sex with *me* occasionally?"

She seemed taken aback by her own assertiveness and sat back down quickly.

We both watched her. Clark finally spoke. "Because you don't want me. That's why," he said, his voice shaky.

The shock on her face mirrored what I felt.

"What? Why would you say that? I'm the one who loves you. I love you so much that I tolerated all those other women so you would be satisfied."

"So you were happy to hand me over to heartless mercenaries who used me like a charge card? You never once objected!"

"I was exhausted, Ethan, taking care of two small boys, taking care of the house, doing your books all those years. I thought I was doing the right thing for all our sakes."

He began to cry. "Holly, why do you stay with me? I'm so fucked and confused. I hate myself. I'm a bad person and you're so good. But I don't understand. When I do want you, why won't you let me make love to you?"

"Why should she?" I said. "You do not hear her, and you treat her like an indentured servant." I stepped in to guide the conversation. "Perhaps because Holly carries a deep resentment for your using so many vacuous women for so long, while she does all the grunt work," I suggested.

Holly sighed. "I suppose that's part of it, Doctor. But the rest is because I'm fat and have bad skin from acne in high school. Sometimes I even find myself gross. Let him have what all successful men want. Beautiful women. Ethan deserves that."

There it was at last. A session in which each one of a couple begins to open their souls, swerving wildly back and forth over the boundaries of their damaged self-esteem.

The breakthrough was exciting. "That is simply not true, Holly. Men want more than beauty. Beauty fades. It's the complexity of couple dynamics that keeps beauty alive," I offered.

"The doctor's right, Holly. You've always been the most beautiful girl in the world to me. I look at you now and see the woman I fell in love with seventeen years ago. I dishonored our vows. I crossed the line."

"Then cross back," I said.

"Holly, you deserved better. G-d, I feel like such a fool!" Ethan began to cry.

"You, Ethan Clark, have been my husband and still are. I don't know how we start over, but I want to honor our vows and feel love for you again."

And then she began to cry.

Luckily, I buy Kleenex in bulk. The sounds of sniffles filled the room. Technically, the session was over, but I would not have ended it for the world.

Ethan stared at his wife as if seeing her for the first time.

"I'm so very, very sorry. I'll do anything to make it up to you. Anything. I'll work with the doctor till I figure out why I allowed all this hurt. I can't lose you. Ever."

He continued to cry as he spoke. She simply listened and, in her intense concern for this flawed man, she was perhaps the most beautiful woman I had ever seen. She slid closer to him on the couch and took his face in her hands, gently stroked his cheeks and then kissed them sweetly.

"OK, Ethan, here's what we have to do: we see Dr. Meyers for as long as it takes and we work hard at our relationship; you tell Frankie to get the fuck out of *your* office and return the money he stole, or you'll report him to the police; and you promise to help me lose ten pounds."

They both laughed.

"If other stuff comes up, we figure it out together. If you agree, kiss me right now." He did kiss her. A long, loving kiss, infused with remorse and hope. It was a magical kiss, and I felt lucky to be a witness.

It had been quite a promising day, and a Saturday no less. On Sunday, my "day off," I would sit down at my dining room table and chart the dynamics of this pair. It was a complicated case and, despite the progress, would be a long, challenging road for all of us; more discovery, triumph and disappointment.

As I sent them off, I suspected they would head for the nearest hotel and get a room.

I gathered my files and packed up. The late-day sun was hitting the buildings with a magical light. People were filling up sidewalk cafes with friends and lovers or rushing past me to get home, to get home to where someone was waiting. I merged with the flow of humanity and was reminded yet again that my life was spent in an office, my clients were my companions, and my adventures were exploring the minds of some pretty bizarre people.

Toward the end of my session with the Clarks, lost feelings of romance stirred in me, watching them find each other again. I remembered my passion for Grace, how it had been part of my daily life. I thought of her throughout each day and couldn't wait to get home to kiss her, inhale her scent, hear about her day and share mine. I decided to walk home. It was time I gave in to the memories. "Physician, heal thyself . . ."

# TWENTY-TWO

A s I walked up West Broadway and into Washington Square Park, I passed couples holding hands. Some stopped to listen to the street musicians, guitarists, a country fiddle player, even an upright bass player. At the far end, bongo drummers provided an infectious beat, the rhythm of the heart.

I had said it a million times over the years: "And this is my wife, Grace." Said with pride and affection. Throughout the early years, even after our sons were born, presenting us with extraordinary challenges, Grace continued to be the beat of my heart. I still loved her passionately even as life continued to morph, became more complicated. But I didn't really have a handle on where we were going.

I had been with one woman my entire life and that was Grace, although I suspected—in fact I knew—that she had been unfaithful to me several times throughout our years together. Why had I turned a blind eye? Perhaps I had convinced myself that it wasn't worth confronting her because the dalliances were harmless, or that the ensuing conflict might disrupt our family life—our children needed rock-solid continuity. Or, truth be told, maybe I wanted to protect my career and that meant preserving the status quo.

The subject finally came up on a spring evening like this a year ago. She suggested we take a walk and "talk." We left the boys with their sitter and headed leisurely downtown toward the northern region of Central Park. Green was everywhere. Dogwood trees were adorned with pink and white flowery balls and azaleas hugged the fronts of brownstones.

We talked as married people do, about the boys and weekend plans. She told me she wanted to cut back on her practice, not deal with the deeply sick, hopeless patients, but take on only those with solvable issues. She told me that she admired how I was able to cope with such varied situations and help so many of the truly damaged patients. And then she brought up her "news."

"I love you, Elias . . ." she began. I sensed a "but" hanging in the air between us. "I'm happy with our life, our children, and I think I'll feel better about things when I make the changes to my practice."

"Feel better about what things," I asked.

"Things. You know . . ."

"No, I don't know unless you actually tell me, Grace."

She slowed her pace and then stopped. We had reached Central Park North. She asked that we sit on a bench on the other side of the street. Things began to feel as if they were moving in slow motion, about to go off the rails.

"Elias, I want more. More travel, adventure, time to myself and—I can't lie to you—I want to take on other lovers."

The clouds had grown darker.

"Well . . ." was all I could muster. "Well, I . . ."

She rushed on. "It's not you, it's me." The cliché of all clichés had just been tossed my way by a fellow professional and the wife I adored.  Only they weren't clichés. Grace needed more, and I could not provide more.

"I don't want a divorce-just a more open marriage."  I looked at Grace, whom I still found sexy and tremendously desirable even after all our years together. Why did she have to look so terrific this particular night?

"You see, Elias, I'm changing. It's nothing you've done."

I sat in silence for quite some time. A taxi drove by and scattered dozens of pigeons into flight.

"But, Grace," I ventured, trying to control my emotions, "your actions, if indeed you take them, will have consequences. What those will be I don't know, but there will be consequences."

"Change is good, Elias. It shakes life up so we don't get too comfortable or bored. Change leads us places we've never been."

"Grace, stop! What if I don't want to go to those places? Change can be good, but you're talking solely about your needs and are not considering ours. This could lead us all down a dark road."

"Or one full of new light!" she insisted.

"If we make changes in our situation, you go traveling, screw around with other men—"

"I didn't say 'screw around.' Don't make me sound vulgar!"

"Then how about fucking other people? Does that work better for you? And travel will take you away from the boys . . ."

"Don't be an ass, Elias. I have the right to do what I want. Marriage is not a prison sentence. I make my own money and can spend it the way I want, and I'd never abandon the boys! They're almost men, in case you hadn't noticed. But I need to find adventure and happiness while I can. You are always working, and studying. You do not live. You're my husband not my warden. I'm trying to be totally honest here. I thought you would appreciate that."

My anger turned icy. "Go home, Grace. I'm going to sit and reflect on all this for a bit." I held out the house keys.

"Elias, we'll talk further. Don't sit here and stew alone. It's about to pour. Come home with me."

I couldn't speak.

"Fine," she said, grabbed the keys, turned on her heel and walked away.

Within minutes there was a clap of thunder that rumbled loud and long. The sky opened up and it rained like a son of a bitch. The downpour washed away a part of my life forever. You didn't have to be a therapist to figure that one out. And then it rained harder and I sat alone on a park bench in a city of millions, all of whom had run for cover.

Sitting there, soaking wet and absolutely paralyzed, I realized there would have to be seismic changes in my life. My marriage to Grace was over, not today or next week, maybe, but within the not too distant future. There was another crack in its foundation and in time the crack would deepen and everything would collapse.

"We don't divorce the people we marry." Those words must have been spoken thousands of times in the offices of counselors, therapists and attorneys. We love the people we wed and over time we change or they do. Circumstances take us on detours and we get lost. We sometimes stay on for the sake of our children, or because of financial considerations. We call it "a bump in the road," make a "fresh start," map out a "new plan" . . . now, "an open marriage." Anything to postpone the inevitable.

In my years of working with couples, I had found that there was very little sense of resolution in divorce. True, there might be a new sense of freedom, but it was ultimately linked to a failed past. When we first started out together, Grace had said many times, "I will enjoy everything you attain, but I will not be responsible for it." I had found it cute and enigmatic when I was young and desperately in love. Now I realized what those words meant.

My life was not over. I would survive. I would make more of an effort to be a better dad and get close to my boys. I would lose myself in my work helping others. Their needs would furnish my life. I would focus on earning even more money to protect myself and my boys from what might come.

I watched people return to the open from under awnings or doorjambs or the giant oak trees at the entrance to the park. I wondered how many of the men would soon be rushing home to their mates as I had just last night. How many would sit down to dinner and look across the table, as I had. I had looked across the table thanking my lucky stars that the woman smiling back at me was the love of my life.

That page in my book had turned. I rose, stiff and clammy, and began to walk uptown. Tomorrow was Sunday. I'd always wanted a dog. I would go out and buy one. I had always wanted a second home in the country. I promised myself I would drive upstate and look for one. I would talk with my boys. The older one was beginning to look at colleges. I wanted to be part of that search. They might need me less and less but I would be there for them more and more. I had probably spent more time with any patient than I had with my boys. That was about to change.

I spent that Sunday in the country with my two boys. I bought my dog, a Kuvasz, whom we named Lazarus, a big, white, sweet, loyal guard dog who bonded with us within minutes. Through a broker friend, we looked at some great houses. I put some earnest money on a bungalow by a lake where we could go fishing together. Suddenly, I was a man of action. I had always been able to help others. Finally, I was going to learn to help myself.

## TWENTY-THREE

I dreamed that I was running with Lazarus in Central Park and woke up thinking how much I missed him now that he lived with Spencer in upstate New York. It was Monday and the sun was just coming up. I had overslept. Most Mondays I got to my office no later than 5:30 a.m. It gave me time to have a coffee and a donut from the all-night diner next door while I pored over my cases for the day. My first appointment was scheduled for seven, in order to accommodate clients who had nine-to-five jobs. I shook off my sleep and my memories and stepped into the shower.

The morning promised a spring rain. A brisk breeze rustled the branches, and the clouds scuttled by. As I approached my office building, I saw from afar that a tall woman was pacing up and down outside the entrance with great agitation. I sped up, somewhat alarmed. When I got closer, I could see that it was Susan Decker.

She called out, "Dr. Meyers, we met Friday afternoon. I was going to call but . . ."

I arrived a bit winded. "Yes, Miss Decker, of course."

She was wearing no makeup. Her auburn hair was somewhat matted and redder than I had remembered. Her eyes were swollen.

"Miss Decker, it's scarcely six and we're not scheduled for an appointment today. Are you all right? Are you in danger?"

"I'm fine," she said. "Well, no, I'm not. I'm sorry to

barge in this morning but I need to talk. I've needed to since Friday night. I'm in real trouble, Doctor."

"Miss Decker, I can't see you right now. I use my Monday mornings to get ready for my day—"

"Doctor, please!"

Her voice was full of panic, her breathing unusually rapid. I backtracked. "But . . . if you'll give me just fifteen minutes to prepare, I'll work you in. Luckily, I don't have a client until eight today."

I gave her a task. "Here's a ten-dollar bill. Please run into that diner next door and buy two glazed donuts. They come out of the oven at just about this time. Bring me a coffee, light and sweet, and get one for yourself. Then come on up to the eighth floor and we'll get started."

She stared at the bill in my hand.

"Miss Decker, I promise those donuts will be worth it, and then we can discuss whatever you need to discuss. OK?"

"Yes, OK." She took the bill and was off on her mission.

Expect the unexpected. Now I had only fifteen minutes to think through a very complex day.

I had Jimmy Sloan, Rebecca and her (G-d help me) Danny Boy, a new patient, and an old one named June Hurley. Each needed focus and deserved my full attention, but I couldn't turn away someone as distressed as Susan Decker.

I heard the elevator and she was back with a half-eaten donut in her hand and a paper bag in the other, looking a lot calmer. She sat on the couch. We both sipped our coffee for a few moments and she began.

"I quit my job over the weekend. I sent a telegram. Didn't even have the guts to say goodbye," she said.

"You could stop by in a week or so, when not so agitated, and say goodbye," I suggested. "But tell me, Miss Decker, what happened since I saw you on Friday?"

She stood and walked around the office like a caged lion, rummaged through her purse and found a cigarette. She lit it and immediately started coughing violently. Crushing it out in the ashtray, she flashed me a whimsical smile. "I don't even smoke."

"Susan, what do you need to tell me?"

And after several minutes she told me the entire saga about her wild, deeply satisfying tryst with Tim.

"Miss Decker," I began.

"Susan," she said. "I want you to call me Susan."

"Why is that important?"

"Because it is, it just is!"

"For now, I will. Susan, it seems that you tested Tim and he passed, so maybe you do have a future with him. But changes in relationships are like ocean liners. They take time to make a turn."

"Are you married, Elias?"

"Yes, but that's not relevant."

"Really? Are you happily married?"

"Again, not appropriate," I said.

"Does your wife see the compassion in your eyes?"

"Miss Decker, unless you share your issues this session is over. Like everyone on this planet, I have issues in my own personal life. But our focus is to heal you. If that's not on your agenda today, we will end this session and I'll recommend another therapist!" (I was running from my conflictual desires. She was into my UCS.)

There was a short pause.

"Tim and I had fantastic sex, like I told you. We spent Friday night together in a warm embrace, but when we got up, something was different. We dressed and had coffee on the corner and read the paper. We spoke very little, you know: tidbits in the news, how nice the weather was and more of the same. We never talked about what had happened the night before nor did we touch at all. We didn't even hold hands or catch each other's gaze. It was a breakfast between two strangers.

"After we paid the bill, Tim asked if it was all right if I walked myself home since he had a busy day.

"'No,' I said. 'You should want to walk me home. I want you to. After what we shared last night, I need you to.'

"There was a long pause. Then he said, 'I don't want to see you anymore, Susan.'

"Just hours ago he'd told me he loved me. I'd offered him a different me, the *real* me, and he seemed to like it . . . and then just hours later, he was leaving me.

"'Tim?' I asked. 'What's wrong? Just hours ago we lay in each other's arms and you told me . . .'

"He said, 'I know what I said, Susan, and I regret saying it. I'm sorry, but your behavior is not what I want from a woman. You're too much. You're . . . just too much. You behaved like an animal. And I can't live with that. There's something . . . off about you and I deserve better.'

"'Something off, Tim? You "deserve better" than the best sex you've ever had? You told me that you—'

"'Susan, you're . . .' He looked away.

"'What, Tim? I'm what?'

"His eyes avoided mine.

"Finally, I said, 'Tim, look at me.'

"He hesitated. 'Look at me!' I demanded.

"And so he did.

"'Susan, you're wild and free. What we did—it scared me. I felt like I was with a whore. It's not normal, what we did.'

"Doctor, I know what we did *was* totally normal. Joyful, even. Jesus, Tim was never going to be right for me. I should've known. He would never offer me what I need or even be curious about what that is. After all the importance I had assigned to him, he turned out to be shallow and afraid.

"All I said was, 'I pity you, Tim,' and headed home. I never looked back."

I gave it a beat of silence to be sure she was finished.

"Well, you had quite a weekend. Wow, you certainly are fearless. Actually, you're worthy of applause."

She looked at me with tears in her eyes and replied with a smile, "Thank you, but why? I wanted it to work. Why am I so fucked up? I blew it again." She began to cry.

I was in a conundrum. Susan had not been on my morning's schedule and my next appointment was minutes away, yet she was on to something about herself that she had never acknowledged. To shut her down was not a good idea.

"Elias, what should I do Thursday night? I can't go to the club anymore, no matter how much I need to. I simply can't go!"

I let her talk.

"But I'm addicted to it all. I'm a fuckin' sex junkie who lives from fix to fix. If I'm alone on Thursday, I'll . . ."

A sob escaped her. She fumbled for a cigarette.

"Susan," I said, "you won't be alone on Thursday. We'll schedule a session at the exact hour you usually visit the club. But this is the deal. You pay for the session, I buy dinner, so don't expect anything expensive. Agreed?"

She looked surprised and enormously relieved. "Yes!" she said. "Eight thirty, where?" (Of course she did not expect that legitimately; I met her UCS needs.)

"There's a quiet place on the corner of Charles and Fourth. I'll be waiting. Don't be late, and bring Minnie Mouse." At her confused look, I pointed to my clock collection. "Mickey needs her back."

She stared into my eyes and said, "You're a life saver, Elias," and before I could protest, her lips grazed my cheek. Then she turned and was gone in a puff of smoke.

I had crossed the line somehow. Not because I had suggested a session over dinner, but because she awakened something in me and I found myself aching for her. (And not her, of course. She awakened the classic wish for "a whore and a Madonna" wrapped up in one from my UCS yearnings, which had always been deflected to one of my aunts from the time I was five.)

# TWENTY-FOUR

Susan Decker passed Jimmy Sloan on her way down the hall. She had left the door ajar so he came into the office without knocking, just as I was downing the rest of my coffee. I greeted him, trying to refocus my energies. He gave me a slight smile and we shook hands. Good, I thought, a firm grip. Although it had been just a few days since I had seen him, Jimmy was somehow different. Slight and fragile, yes; he might still break like a chicken bone. Yet his aura had changed. Steely was the best way to describe it, edgy.

He sat on the couch, his posture erect.

"Hello, Dr. Meyers." He took off his thick glasses. He rubbed his eyes with such intensity I imagined they might have been erased by the time he put his glasses back on. Then he relaxed on the sofa and crossed his right leg over his left. It bounced a bit to a silent beat of agitation.

"How's your mother?" I asked.

"Improving."

And then he said nothing. Nothing, absolutely nothing, for the next fifty minutes.

He stood to go. "See you next week, Dr. Meyers." And he too was gone in a puff of smoke.

I paced the office and reflected on Jimmy's puzzling behavior. His energy and demeanor seemed to be in a passive-aggressive war with each other. He was on his own now, his father deceased, his mother estranged. Perhaps he was feeling a void since the constant demands of his mother had been removed. There would potentially be more silent sessions before he was ready to articulate the tangle of emotions that filled his head and broken heart. Maybe he was somehow working things out in my presence. Jimmy's dilemma was like a giant jigsaw puzzle missing many crucial pieces.

It was close to my mid-morning break. Usually I would take a walk around the block, get some air and clear my head. That was my daily ritual, no matter the weather. But because of Susan Decker's surprise visit I decided to stay in and catch up. Just as I was finishing, my new patient arrived.

He was a police officer from a precinct some hundred blocks away, a tall, sturdy man of six feet or more with a barrel chest and muscular arms. Although he had a young face, I guessed he was close to fifty by the gray streaks in his sandy hair.

He offered a handshake and a salute. "Captain Greenspan, NYPD. Thank you for seeing me, Doctor." I indicated the couch. "I believe I'm going through some sort of episode."

"Episode?"

"I had the precinct send over the file. Did you read it?" he asked.

"Yes I did, Captain. Please continue."

"The word 'hero' . . . how is that defined in your line of work, Doctor?" He sat at attention on the coach as if he were about to be interrogated.

I chose my words carefully. "Saving lives while risking your own. Taking out evil and leaving goodness in its place. From what the PD psychiatrist reported in your files, that's exactly what you did. Do you disagree with that assessment?"

"Correct," he answered, "I disagree."

"Really? You single-handedly derailed a major bank robbery in which four adults and two children were held hostage and the bank manager was brutally killed. You received the NYPD Medal of Honor. How is that not heroic?"

Another F. Scott Fitzgerald quote popped into my head: "Show me a hero and I will write you a tragedy."

"I was taken off the job to recover from what they said was trauma for six months! Heroes don't receive desk jobs! They return to the field and continue to protect our citizens. How many persons are being damaged by my being chained to a desk?" He was suddenly livid; I was caught off guard by his unstable behavior.

"Captain, you might not have been physically injured in this incident, but your mind may have been. It takes just as much time to heal from shock as it takes to heal from a gunshot wound, sometimes even longer."

"You take me for a fool, Doctor?" He was shouting, trembling. I had the instinct that something was about to happen. Could I beat him to the door?

I stopped that thought. A memory flashed before me. During World War II all my uncles would gather on Sundays to practice shooting rifles and handguns. There was a large long basement filled with coal bins and several adjacent rooms. Part of the family was already exterminated in some concentration camp in Poland. The family was fierce. All my uncles were longshoremen. Weapons and ammunition never seemed to be a problem. All were illegal. The family had come to some agreement that if Brooklyn were invaded, they would fight to the death.

I was quite young. I felt the spirit. Death did not have such meaning then. I was given a rifle, which I could not lift. I still have it. There were twenty-two adults, mostly male, plus older cousins. After shooting and cleaning up the basement, everyone retired to the upstairs parlor for food. The women always cooked while the men practiced.

I remembered my grandfather was a blacksmith and that the kids and he fought their way through central Europe with knives and short swords hand-made by my grandfather. So, there I was.

Suddenly, the captain stood and pulled a snub-nosed thirty-eight from his right hip and placed it loudly on the table. "You cure me, Doctor, and *now*, or I'll shoot you before I leave this office." He sat down calmly and waited for me to answer his challenge.

I grabbed my chest and leaned forward, faking pain. Before he could react, I had pulled my Kimber from its holster and was pointing it at his chest. "No one is shooting anyone, Captain. I don't want a worthy life like yours to end in a spray of bullets and a legacy of shame. And I have no intention of ending up dead."

He registered amazement and raised his hands. He was smart; my weapon outgunned him by a lot.

I removed his gun from the table, placed it in my desk drawer and locked it. Keeping my gun trained on his chest, I took out my bottle of Maker's Mark and poured two shots. A little early in the day, but this was no ordinary day.

"Drink this, Captain, and then let's talk about what demons are driving you to destruction. Deal?"

"Deal," he said softly.

With the bottle between us, we drank. Minutes passed and I found myself sharing the story of how Frank Todd tried to kill me, injuring my police escort. How killing him had been both a blessing and a curse. I could see that he looked at me differently. Within the context of a police action, I seemed more like a kindred spirit.

Finally, I lowered my gun and returned it to its holster. Quietly, I asked how I could help him. His shoulders began to shake with the release of tension. I waited until he was breathing normally enough to talk.

"Three weeks ago I returned to active duty. Because of my rank, I received the right to make rounds solo, in my own patrol car as I had prior to the incident at the bank. Nothing of particular note happened over the first two weeks. Gangs and other troublemakers dispersed at the sight of my car or the burst of its siren. Sometimes I parked and walked into off-the-beaten-path streets in the Village; up West Street by the river, or down to Soho and the financial district. I worked the midnight to 8 a.m. shift and everything went fine. I made a few simple collars. Drug busts where there was no resistance, just some schmucks in the wrong place at the wrong time. I shut down a bar serving to underage kids and handled a domestic violence. Same routine every night."

Without asking, he poured himself another shot of Maker's Mark and I watched him down it for courage. His faced flushed. I sensed it was not from the alcohol, but from some deep-rooted embarrassment he felt because of something he was about to tell me.

"As you may know, there's a great deal of gay bashing in the Village. Most of the gay bars are on Grove, Christopher and West. Most of them are located in darkened alleys that splinter off into backyard entrances or side doors. These g-ddamn faggots! They fuck up my city. Just keep your cock in your g-ddamn pants, get a room or jack off in the bathroom!" He was sounding irrational again. He caught himself and regained control. "Anyway, over the years my officers and I have collared a great many perps beating up on those poor fags.

"Three nights ago while on patrol I discovered—stumbled upon a gay bashing off of Barrows, taking place in a hidden area between two old brownstones. I stopped the cruiser and focused its spotlight into the alleyway. There were three men with their pants down forcing a man they were holding down to perform oral sex on them."

I said nothing and it irritated the captain. "Did you hear me?" he shouted.

"Yes," I replied, "go on."

"And then I realized, it wasn't a gay bashing it was a fucking faggot orgy." He nearly gagged and stopped speaking. His words filled the air like a heavy dark cloud. I became aware of the tick of the clocks on my desk. "I pulled my gun and told the men to stand with their hands over their heads. Three pulled up their trousers and did as they were told. The fourth man turned onto his stomach and looked over his shoulder at me without any fear.

"'Hey officer,' he said, 'put that gun away, why don't you? You don't want to arrest us, especially me. Just giving these boys a little pleasure—a good time. We all need one now and then don't we, even big strong cops in their fancy uniforms. Right? I know you're the boss, sir. Just tell me what to do and I'll do it. Come on, sweetie, boss me around.'

"I was pissed but I kept my cool. 'That's enough, son. Mocking the law isn't going to get you out of the trouble you're already in. So zip it! Shut the fuck up and do what I told you to do."

The captain's eyes glazed over as he took on the extremely gay demeanor of the man in his story. "'Oh, Captain, you're so *hot* when you boss me around. Do it some more! Boss me, you big hunky man!' He said this as he got up and walked toward me. His pants were unzipped and his cock stood at attention through his zipper. And then, and then . . . I collapsed. I did not know what possessed me. I could not shoot. I never thought of clubbing him. I never thought I needed help, back up. My mind was a blank. I was far away and yet right there. I was paralyzed, helpless.

His pain was so overwhelming, it felt like an anvil on my chest. And he was going to fall deeper into his personal Hades unless I slowed him down somehow . . .

"They took turns. *Took turns* and I let them. When they were done, they got dressed and left me lying there sobbing. 'See you at the Glory Hole, Captain Homo!' They ran away but I couldn't move. Somehow I made it home and vomited all night. I hate myself! My wife is dead. I am a good Christian. I need to die!"

"Captain, you're in shock. Please breathe, slow down a little—"

He didn't hear me. "I didn't report the incident and called in sick the next two days. Then I asked around saying that 'my friend' needed a shrink. Someone gave me your name. I asked that they send over my files since I would be coming to the sessions with 'my friend.' I'm a Christian, and a widower who has dishonored my wife. I'm a cop and I'm a fag. I'm a fucking deviate fag who has betrayed my G-d and my family. I'm done, Doctor. It's OVER FOR ME!"

He completely collapsed. He needed immediate medical attention. I leaned over him to be sure he was breathing. In a flash, his eyes flew open and he grabbed my lapels.

"Now give me back my gun! My life is no longer worth living. Give me my gun!" He screamed like a wounded animal and his hand felt my Kimber under my jacket. I pulled back and tried to break free. He lunged forward. His strength was epic, driven by madness. He overwhelmed me and wrested my gun from its holster. I grabbed his wrists and we wrestled to the floor with both our lives on the line.

## TWENTY-FIVE

Susan Decker left Elias's office with much of her fear and anxiety replaced by some sort of ephemeral good feeling. It was the first Monday in almost fourteen years that she didn't have to show up for work. More importantly, she felt safe and not completely alone. Elias Meyers understood her lifetime of solitude and self-censorship, the burden of knowing that she would be ostracized if she gave up her terrible secret. She couldn't bear it anymore. Not that he could solve all her woes overnight, but she finally had a partner in her effort to heal. She felt hopeful and that hope made her smile.

She headed uptown to the Plaza and had an expensive breakfast of eggs benedict, caviar and three Bloody Marys. She was more than a little lit when she paid the bill—over a hundred dollars. Price be damned! She walked into the early summer morning and headed across the street to Henri Bendel's and ordered a deluxe spa treatment. When it was finished some three hours later, all twenty of her nails glistened bright red, her skin glowed and she was sporting a new hairstyle that made her look girlish, which was exactly how she felt.

Her next stop was Bergdorf's where she spent a month's pay on a black cocktail dress that hugged her so close it left little to the imagination, and bought three inch heels and sexy, sheer-black patterned stockings. And then she sat at the makeup counter for a "makeover" with an Asian cosmetician who sculpted her cheeks with coral blush, applied a deep, rosy lipstick and mascara that made her lashes look like butterfly's wings. All those years her mother had made her feel homely and unwanted. What a cold bitch. And if only her father could see her now!

Then she walked over to the park and hired a horse-drawn carriage for a two-hour ride through Central Park. As she paid the driver she realized that in her fourteen years in NY she had never even been to Central Park. She sat back and relaxed to the clip-clop of the horse's shoes on the pavement and began to think through her life with renewed perspective.

She was a smart, mature woman, not some teenager with a crush. Yet that was how she felt when she thought about Elias Meyers. She knew what she planned to wear was inappropriate for her session with him on Thursday. Perhaps she would change her mind and dress down, but for the moment she was happy and her fear of "going to the club" seemed to have been washed away by the midday breeze that smelled like lilac and fresh cut grass. She watched the denizens of the city as her coach took her through places unknown. She asked the driver to linger by the carousel and watched the joy in the faces of the children as they lived in the moment without fear of the future.

The coach took her by softball games played by people of varying ages. In one field, young boys and girls played an informal game of soccer, flirting with one another as the ball passed among their tan, muscular legs. She wanted to be caught up in that world of innocent dreams and possibilities. She was determined to fix what was broken, become a new person. *Why not?* she thought. *This park is filled with people who live wearing smiles; why can't I be one of them?*

The work she needed to do on herself would begin in earnest when she met with Elias Meyers for dinner tomorrow night. She promised herself that she would act like a patient and not a flirt. She needed his guidance and compassion and, despite what she felt when she looked into his eyes, she wanted his wisdom more than his heart. (Smart woman, correct evaluation.)

{}

Rules of therapy: the patient had to take the lead. But he had hoped that, just for today, the doctor would take the lead and talk to him first. All the thoughts that Jimmy wanted to express had frozen in his throat. Toward the end of his session, he began to realize that he wanted the doctor talk to him in his father's voice, the voice that had been the buffer for the harsh world of his childhood: the bullying, the disappointment when Sue Ellen Edwards, who lived next door, wouldn't play with him, the darker episodes in middle school when Todd Edgerton held his head in the toilet and some sidekick kept flushing.

Jimmy realized that his kind father had unwittingly enabled him to continue seeing himself as a victim. He realized that his mother had been trying to compensate for all Jimmy's wounds in her own desperation to fill the void once her husband had died. But it didn't matter what he realized or didn't realize. Jimmy was a person who attracted bad things and somehow deserved them. A surge of determination seized him. He had to get uptown to see the Monets before the Metropolitan Museum closed.

His father had taken him there many times when he was growing up. They had sat side by side studying "Water Lilies," walked among the various paintings examining the master's tiny brush strokes up close, and then had stood far away, taking in their enormous effect. His father was the ultimate tour guide of his life, the one who could explain something from every angle, whether it was a painting or puberty.

He reached the museum only to find that it was closed. Of course, it was Monday. He knew that! He stood for a few minutes waiting for the doors to blow open from the force of his need. But they did not. Cautiously, he found his way down the stairs, his eyes clouded with tears.

At the bottom of the stairs, a seller of used books sat in a folding chair having a smoke, oblivious to the beauty under his fingertips. Jimmy noticed a coffee table edition of Picasso's *Guernica Studies* and a biography of Renoir. Wedged underneath was a smaller book, the corner a smudge of luminous turquoise and pink. His pulse quickened as he lifted it out. *The Impressionists* was dog-eared but, even with his poor eyesight, he could identify every one of the prints. He paid the vendor and walked downtown toward his old haunt, the art store on 57th. It had been a long time since he had bought painting supplies, a long time since he had experienced anything but fear and confusion. Tonight he would paint water lilies.

# TWENTY-SIX

I didn't stand a chance against the police captain. He outweighed me by at least thirty pounds and his superior muscularity was enhanced by desperation.

"Captain, stop it!" I shouted again and again.

Briefly, I evaded his grasp and struggled to my feet. He was up in a flash, grabbed the back of my neck and tossed me aside as if I were a rag doll. Simultaneously, he kicked the top of my knee cap with his boot and caused my leg to hyperextend. The pain was unbearable. I lost my grip on the pistol and fell, writhing on the floor. He stood and glowered down at me. Certainly within moments I would be dead.

"Captain, killing me will not make your pain go away!"

Holding the pistol by his side, he used his other hand to straighten his uniform as if readying for inspection from a superior. His breathing became measured and the manic expression slowly faded. His superego and ego kicked in. He looked somewhat puzzled.

"Are you hurt"? he asked.

("Of course, you crazy fuck. You busted my knee, you Looney Toon!" I didn't actually say that but I wanted to.)

"Yes, I'm hurt," I managed through clenched teeth.

He offered his hand. I took it and, in a single motion, he pulled me from the floor and onto my chair. Still moaning, I cautiously stretched my leg. Apparently, nothing was broken but it would be a long time before I walked without a limp.

He sat across from me expectantly as he had when he first arrived. It was as though time had rewound and the wrestling match had never happened. I rolled up my pant leg and looked at my swollen knee.

"I apologize for hurting you. I didn't know that was going to happen."

When I looked up I saw he had my Kimber pointed right between my eyes. "I didn't see where you put my gun, Doctor. I want it back right now. Right now. And then I'll do what I need to do and you'll be safe."

"What is it you need to do, Captain?" I asked, already knowing the answer.

"Kill myself."

I had to improvise fast. "First I must ask your assistance. There's an icepack in the fridge. I can't walk. Please bring me the ice pack." As a matter of fact, my knee was beginning to throb.

He stared at me in disbelief.

"You must be crazy, Doctor. Give me my gun or I'm going to shoot you!"

"*I'm* crazy? You're the one who came here for my help and are about to shoot me for trying. You're the one about to destroy your legacy and bring shame upon all you know. And *I'm* crazy? Why don't you give that a second thought? If you shoot me, how will you know where I put your gun? Now GET THE ICEPACK and put my fucking gun down!"

He was confused by my reaction but he didn't budge. I needed to buy more time. "Hey, Captain, you think you're a smart guy, right?"

He actually thought before he answered.

"Yes."

144

"Well then act like one! If you shoot me, you'll never find your gun. And, by the way, do you think that in this entire world you're the only one who finds themselves lost? The only one?"

Again he thought before he answered.

"I imagine that's not actually possible," he replied.

"*To err is human; to forgive, divine.* Have you ever heard that?"

He hesitated. "Of course."

"Say it!" I shouted

"*To err is human; to forgive, divine.*"

"Say it again!" I demanded. He repeated the adage with more conviction. The pendulum was swinging back. "Now get me the fucking icepack. Then sit down and let's work on forgiveness!"

At last he moved and, within moments, I had an icepack on my knee and the Kimber rested on the table between us. I prayed that the safety was still on. The threat was far from over so I took the lead. He had just had a primitive, totally psychotic episode, so acute I could hardly believe it was isolated. And yet his superiors had put him back on active duty. Had they not picked up on his unstable behavior?

"Captain, you must understand that your actions of the other night were likely an anomaly. Your life has recently been confusing, stressful beyond belief, filled with danger."

"No excuses. I put a man's cock in my mouth. I let a man put his in my ass and I was aroused. I'm a fag, and being a fag is something I can't live with."

"Stonewall was fifteen years ago. The world has changed. You need to consider that you may have changed too without realizing it. If you had closed your eyes and imagined the pleasure you received was from beautiful women would you be as upset?"

"It wasn't! It was from dirt bag faggots." He was becoming agitated again. My attempt to rationalize was no good.

"Captain, please agree to come to me on a regular basis so I can help you; and I know I can. If for no other reason than to help me with my wrestling skills. You have to admit I could use some work."

Then he laughed. "Damn straight, Doctor. Damn fuckin' straight."

And then we both laughed. Even lame humor can trump fear.

"Captain," I said, wiping away tears, "we can make this right. It's close to five. I need a break. Let's meet back here at seven. You and I can talk till dawn. We're going to start putting this incident in perspective. Go take in a movie, eat something. At seven, we get to work, OK?"

His brow furrowed but he said, "OK."

I finally exhaled. He looked at my gun but didn't touch it.

"Great! See you later."

"Deal, Doctor", he replied, "I'll see you later." And he left.

Once he stepped into the elevator, I closed the door and called 911. When I explained the situation, I was transferred to a supervisor. I requested that police come down to 11th street as soon as possible, find the captain and get him to St. Vincent's. Although he was unarmed, I warned them that force might be necessary. Then I collapsed into my chair, my knee the size of a grapefruit, but I was relieved and happy. Within hours, the captain would be sedated and out of harm's way. The last shot of Maker's Mark hit the spot. I was thrilled be part of saving the soul of a deeply troubled man.

I looked out the window. Captain Greenspan waited at

the bus stop along with another dozen New Yorkers headed uptown. I hated tricking him but I knew it was my only hope of saving him. Although he had kicked the shit out of me physically and emotionally, I liked the guy. I wanted to help him come to terms with himself. Hopefully, the police would be arriving any moment. I could see his bus rounding the corner. Well, if he got on, they knew where they could find him later at seven in my office.

The captain moved to the front of the line, jostling a woman with two big bags of groceries. And then, just as the bus pulled up, he stepped in front of it. Everyone screamed. The driver jumped out and got on his knees, looking under the bus. From his body language I could see that the captain was beyond help, no longer a person with a history or a future. The police cars, three of them, were coming down the block. They screeched to a halt and the first person to jump out was my former guardian, Officer Stone.

I had failed to help save a soul. With the senseless death of this good man . . . Well, everything changed.

# TWENTY-SEVEN

I stood motionless and, despite my desire to look away, I couldn't stop watching the chaos that the police captain's suicide had caused. His death was not his alone. It would be a nightmare those witnesses would never forget. And the driver's life was forever tarnished. Even though it was not his fault, that death would forever be on his hands. Taking your own life might mean ending your own pain, but it leaves terrible scars on the lives left behind.

My intuition had clearly failed this time. I tore myself away as the ambulance pulled up and walked slowly to the sink in the back of the office. I looked in the mirror at the tired old man looking back at me. Then I started to sob.

I was in no condition to help anyone. I seriously needed help myself. I paged all my patients who were on my schedule and canceled their appointments, changed my shirt and took several aspirin to dull the pain in my knee. I replaced my gun in its shoulder holster and took the captain's gun out of the locked drawer. Then I turned off the lights, locked the door and limped toward the elevator.

Officer Stone was surprised to see me approaching him; even more so when I gave him a synopsis of events and handed him the captain's gun. He patted my shoulder. "Sorry, Doc. You OK?" My eyes filled with tears. I had no other answer but to walk away. Traffic was backed up due to the tragedy. Ten blocks from my office I was finally able to hail a cab.

I felt a compelling need to talk to Grace. Since the "open marriage" arrangement, my relationship with her had been strained at best. As my relationships with my sons had grown closer, the distance between us had been widening. This morning's awful events made me want to rethink the situation. She was still my wife. I still held love in my heart for her and perhaps her need to "live a different life" was not narcissism, but a path to a happier, more fulfilled existence.

No one knew better than I how easily life could end between your last breath and the next. Day after day, I sat in my chair reflecting on the turmoil of the tortured souls who sought me out and trusted me . . . as if I led such an exemplary life! I desperately needed to be connected with someone who cared about me—just Elias the man.

Grace would most likely be home from work. She would listen to what had happened and know the right thing to say. I would throw away my bitter self-righteousness and conventional thinking and just maybe we could rekindle the days we had spent under a cobalt sky and a neon sun of the past. Something good had to come of this tragic day.

But as I entered the apartment I heard noises coming from the bedroom. I froze. They were giddy, lustful sounds.

"Grace?" I called.

Then I heard indecipherable heated whispers. I knew what I'd find when I walked into the bedroom but I hoped against hope I'd be wrong. Of course, I wasn't.

Grace was naked in bed with some stranger easily ten years her junior. Stunned, I watched my wife, my own *wife*, hold up a sheet to cover her nakedness. What did she think she was hiding from me? The schmuck next to her was some big gorilla with a hairy chest and muscles on top of muscles. The absurdity of it made me smile at the folly of my thoughts on the way home—how I had planned to swoop in and put my humpty-dumpty marriage back together again. All the king's men couldn't have achieved that now. Whatever it was that had gotten me home began to crumble.

"Elias, what are you doing here?" Grace asked as if it was her party and I had not been invited.

"I live here. It's my home. This is my bedroom. That's my bed. You want to take other lovers, do it in someone else's bed, not mine. Were you planning to change the sheets before you slept next to me tonight or is this schmuck planning on staying?"

"Hey, show some fuckin' resect!" said the ape.

"I find you in my bed with my wife and I should show you respect? Christ, Grace! This gorilla has a vocabulary of six words and a comb-over? What happened to you, Grace?"

Ape-man got out of the bed with a towel barely covering him and got into my face. "Maybe if you fucked your wife now and then, she wouldn't need someone like me, you little faggot." (Maybe true, too involved in work, I ran away from the very intimacy I showed easily in my work.)

I had heard enough of the word faggot today to last a lifetime. The situation was so pathetic, I started to laugh. That made the ape-man angry. "Hey, shut up!" he shouted. "What you laughing at anyway?"

"Elias, stop!" she pleaded.

That only made me laugh harder. I looked at Grace, who was no longer attempting to cover herself. "You are such a cliché. I mean, this guy is such a dope! What do you do when he finishes fucking you? Talk about his grade school education?" Rage was rising in me; my primitive limbic system was controlling my mouth. "The size of his dick?" (My rage, my despair, my very old fantasies crushed.)

With that comment, ape-man slapped me across the face.

"Get out, little man, before I have to hurt you!"

"Nope, that is not going to happen, shit for brains." And with that I took the Kimber from its holster and put two shots into the plaster wall behind the bed. The bullets whizzed by his ear with the barrel so close to his face that it left powder burns. The sound was so deafening I thought he might shit his pants if he were wearing any.

Grace shrieked. "What, are you crazy? Elias! Are you fucking crazy?"

I pointed the gun at his crotch. "Get out. Now. No time to get dressed. Out now or the next shot takes your dick off and you bleed to death on my floor."

He grabbed his clothes and ran. No further discussion.

I turned to my wife. "No, Grace, I'm not crazy. If I were crazy, you and Tarzan would both be dead."

"Elias." She broke down. "We had an arrangement, Elias. I didn't think you'd be home this early."

I looked at my naked wife and all the love I had felt for her evaporated. Suddenly I was exhausted.

She wiped her tears on the bedsheet. "I can't stay with you, Elias, I need a new life."

"Good," I said. "GO! Stop talking about this new life and go live it somewhere else. Whatever we had is over."

"What are you going to do, Elias?" Now she was sobbing.

"Well, I'm going to remove the bullets from the wall and spackle and repaint my bedroom. But first I'm going to burn these sheets and replace them with some brand new ones. When I return from the store, I expect you to be gone. Anything you leave behind, I will put in garbage bags at the side of the house. And then, Grace, I'm going to take a nap on my new sheets and forget I ever knew you."

(No one to talk to, to listen to my harrowing day, my doubts about my work—gone with another tragedy.)

Despite my bravura, I was shaken to the core. I left the house with my heart broken, my mind a swirling kaleidoscope of dark thoughts, and my sense of loss so overwhelming that I found it difficult to walk. I saw my soon to be ex-wife's boyfriend in a parking lot a half a block from our building trying to scramble into his clothing between parked cars. I wanted to feel the satisfaction of revenge but it was all too grotesque. I was a man who had just been cuckolded by his wife in his own home with a human ape. I hurried past, obsessed with buying clean sheets for my new life.

The bed and bath store was just a few blocks away. The shop girl was in her early twenties with crazy, frizzy red hair that had a life all its own. Her smile was a beacon.

"How can I help you, sir?"

"Sheets," I said. "I want to buy the most expensive cotton sheets you sell and I want them to be bright and bold and . . . reckless."

She walked to the back of the store and returned shortly with three different choices. "These are all top of the line, sir. The best money can buy!"

The orange and yellow set was the most expensive and the color was the brightest—I'd need sunglasses to sleep. The sales girl was eager to help. "These are Egyptian, thousand-count, so they'll last a lifetime." Then she went on to explain what the "count" meant. I imagined a thousand Egyptians sewing under a hot desert sun with the pyramids standing tall and proud behind them.

I paid the young lady, a sweetheart, and she thanked me with a sincere, "Thank you, sir, I hope your purchase brings you great happiness."

I smiled. The definition of happiness is "contentment, pleasure or joy arising from circumstances or events." So it was hard to "have happiness." And if one could have it, it would always be something one could lose. One could rationalize, put one's personal events into context, or gain perspective. But happiness, one could not manufacture. Today I had lost both a patient and a wife but I did have clean sheets; clean, Egyptian, thousand-count orange and yellow sheets.

## TWENTY-EIGHT

When I arrived home Judith was sitting on the stoop outside of our building. Judy was the landlord's daughter. I saw her now and then with several preschoolers in tow. I vaguely knew that she ran a state-supported daycare upstairs for kids who had inherited HIV. We had once exchanged casual pleasantries in the local market where she was purchasing a half-dozen boxes of graham crackers for their snacks.

I had never found her particularly attractive, but now, as I approached, I realized that my life had changed. Although I had never wanted to participate in an "open marriage," the universe had suddenly granted permission. For all intents and purposes I was newly single. Maybe Grace had handed me an opportunity I would never otherwise have known.

Judy seemed to have been waiting for me and greeted me with an awkward hug. "Is everything OK? We heard gunshots and ran down. I saw Grace run out with a suitcase. Dad and I let ourselves in to be sure no one was hurt. Should I call the police?"

She was a petite woman close to forty with shoulder-length, mousey-brown hair and a gymnast's body. Her smile was easy and her laugh quick to follow. She was pleasant looking in a kind of sisterly way, still wearing her work jeans and a baggy tee shirt, tie-dyed with juice stains.

"No! Everything's under control now. Thank you for your concern, Judy." I was certain that I sounded like a cranky professor after a day of classes during which all his lectures fell flat.

"Elias, there was this really built guy waiting in a cab. They ran in and out taking stuff with them. I think she maybe, like, ran away with him. I'm really sorry."

"Judy, I'm not able to have this conversation right now." And with that I brushed her aside and entered the building.

As the door closed behind me I heard her call out. "Hey, Dr. Meyers, I'll be here for a while if you change your mind."

I stopped and opened the door. She was being kind which, if today was any measure, was a rarity in this world.

"Thanks, Judy. Thanks. Do you have a session rate?"

She smiled. "My first one is free and depending on your needs we'll discuss the fee." And then she winked.

"Fair enough."

"Hey, maybe you just need someone to take you for a quick bite?" she said like a concerned mom.

"Not a good time, Judy." I was exhausted. And then in a heartbeat I turned back. "How about tomorrow at 7:00?"

"OK," she said, pleasantly surprised, "Yeah, Tuesday is Ladies Night at Lucy's. You're on!" I nodded and went inside.

The apartment was a bit like a spook house. Spencer and Rodney were away at excellent boarding schools upstate and doing well. I had ordered Grace gone and indeed she was gone with the wind. Nothing of her remained. Not even her scent. It was if she had pre-packed and was ready to bolt; as if a genie had come and Grace had used her remaining wish to disappear. No photos left behind, no wall hangings, or even her dishes. Her books were gone as well. Dozens of them. Packed willy-nilly into a taxi and all rolling away to some destination unknown.

She had stripped the bed. The soiled sheets lay on the floor. Was that a sign of respect or contempt? She had written a note on the bedroom mirror in red lipstick. "Thanks for the ride, Elias. It was fun at times. You were quite 'The Man.' Find peace. Be healthy." Around it she had drawn a heart. I stared at the message written in deep red. Then I proceeded to wipe it away, the message and the remnants of the woman. It was like pulling the plug on life support.

I sat on the bed, my back straight and my hands folded in my lap. Then I got up and dressed my bed with thousands of Egyptian threads, obscenely bright yellow and orange, promising a better day than the one I had just lived through.

As I reclined, my heart rate jumped. I realized that in order to be free of Grace, I would need to buy a new mattress, maybe a whole new bed. But it was getting on toward evening. I remained still and breathed as I had when Grace and I were receiving training in Lamaze class. Cleansing, deep inhalations, short rhythmic exhalations. I reached over and turned on the radio. Sinatra was singing, cool as ever, "Cry Me a River."

I did as I was told and began to weep.

I fell asleep, woke sweating, fell asleep, got up to take a pill, and sat on the couch thinking. I had once written a letter to my oldest son who was having a crisis of the soul, having been rejected from some ridiculous fraternity for not being "the right kind of man" for them.

I had written something to this effect: "A real man is courageous yet not foolish, thinks strategically and does not act out of impulse. He has compassion for others, for without such a trait he is but a shallow robot that can care for no one and will live a life devoid of love, loss or joy. Yet this man must love himself first.

"Move forward now. You are better than those who have chosen not to embrace you. Be generous and courageous. Work for your goals with commitment. Get up and get up again to carry the ball down the field. Love and know you too will be loved. You are loved now, son. Dad."

# TWENTY-NINE

June Hurley was waiting for me outside my office when I arrived the next morning just prior to 7 a.m. I was surprised to see her since her appointment was much later. I was surprised and not pleased. June had always been a difficult patient when I was at my best. Today I was awash in gray, having spent a sleepless night thinking of every event or action I had taken or encountered throughout my lifetime. No matter how I rearranged the potential outcomes or different results in my head my reality was what it was. Both wishful thinking and regret were pointless.

Despite my dismay at her unscheduled presence June Hurley looked great. She always looked great . . . ready for action, knowing how to turn heads when entering a room and knowing how to use her sexuality to control a situation. She had been a patient on and off for years and I never saw any change in her or any desire to change.

June came to see me with the hope of justifying her behaviors, or so she told me. I tried to help her see why her life was crowded with people, activity and even adventure, but she always ached with loneliness. Everywhere she went, with whomever, and whatever she chose to do was ultimately unfulfilling because she didn't trust anyone, therefore could not bond. A life without love is cold existence. I would remain her doctor, but my hope for her to see the light diminished each time she made her way back to my office between absences.

"June, you don't have an appointment today and I'm backed up, so call if it's urgent and I'll fit you in when I can." With that I brushed by her and into the lobby, waiting for the elevator to come and save me from any sort of confrontation.

"Elias, it *is* urgent, otherwise I wouldn't be waiting at this ungodly hour to see you. It simply can't wait!"

She said all that as if it were rehearsed; as if she knew I'd say yes and squeeze her in. But after the disaster of the captain's suicide, I was not emotionally capable of dismissing anyone who might be in need. I unlocked the elevator and we got in. June stood too close and smelled of some sickly sweet, expensive perfume. When I unlocked my office, she headed straight for the couch. I hung my sport coat on the back of the door, opened the window to mitigate her heavy scent and put on a pot of coffee.

When I sat in my chair and turned to face June she was half naked. She had removed the blazer she'd been wearing and unbuttoned her expensive silk blouse, exposing her large breasts. She had let her hair down and it tumbled over her shoulders, auburn as an Irish setter's, and sat with her bare feet tucked under her ass, revealing that she was without panties.

Even more surprising was the small leather overnight bag that sat upside down on the table, its contents strewn randomly about: bottles of prescription drugs, bags of marijuana, sex toys and cash. It was stunning to see stacks of hundreds with Ben Franklin's serious expression staring back at the crack of dawn. I poured myself a cup of coffee. I didn't offer any to June.

"I'm charging you for this session, June. I have no idea what you're up to, so let's have it. I have no time or inclination for games."

"I came because I care for you, Elias."

Unintentionally, I scoffed. "June, I know you. I don't believe you care about anyone unless you benefit from it. So, with all due respect, I very much doubt your motives."

"Well, I do care. You know you were all over the news the other night? 'The police captain had just left Dr. Elias Meyers's office before jumping in front of a bus.' Not great for business. You're in trouble and I'm here to help you out of it. See, I do care!"

"It shows motive, not concern, June. But I'm sure when you reveal how you intend to 'help me' there'll be something in it for you."

She stood up and dropped her blouse to the floor. She was now buck-naked from the waist up. "Why don't you fuck me, Elias? Have some fun. Let me give you pleasure. Someone has to."

What was her game? "You've crossed the line, June. I'll find you someone else to see. We're done. You owe me two hundred dollars for this session."

She ignored me and crossed the room, pressed her naked body into mine and began to rub herself against me. I was aroused. I was angry. But I wasn't confused.

I pushed her away. She slapped me across the face.

"You schmuck, Elias. You stupid, lonely schmuck. The all-knowing Dr. Elias Meyers's practice is going to take a hit because that stupid cop killed himself after he left your office. Stop being a g-ddamned martyr and let me help you!"

"How is this pathetic seduction going to help me? I'm a doctor in real life, not an actor in some film noir fantasy in your twisted mind!"

I immediately regretted the words, a violation of my professional code, but then I was not feeling well. This was all too much too soon after a night of self-analysis and grief.

June was relentless. She lay down on the couch and spread her legs wide. (I honestly felt revolted, ice cold to this commercial seduction. I was enraged, and deeply offended.)

"Come on, Elias, fuck me. It will help you live longer."

I grabbed the chenille throw that rested on the club chair and threw it over her naked body.

"Get dressed, June, and then leave. As I said, I'll find you another doctor."

I picked up the phone.

"Operator, this is Dr. Meyers. Please connect me to the police."

June lunged at the phone and ripped the cord from the wall.

"You haven't heard my deal yet. Why do you have to be such an ass?"

"Get dressed now. I'll give you five minutes before I open that window and scream for a cop. Talk, June. Your time is running out."

She picked up her clothes with a sneer. "You would have listened better after a good fuck." She began to button her blouse. "OK, so you know Walter—"

Now June was fully dressed, seated in a civilized manner. My heart still raced but I had regained my professional composure. The clocks ticked. Once my terms were met, once she sat fully clothed opposite me, I gestured that she begin.

"I'm working with Walter Brennan. You know him, right?"

I nodded.

"We've developed a brilliant plan to sell drugs like these that are spread out on your table to high-end patients. We'll make tens of thousands a week. All we want— for *double* what you make in this little room—all we want is your *silence*. Nothing else. Don't rat him out and you'll make more in a month than you make in a year. Everyone wins! And if you get off your high horse I'll fuck you whenever you need a vacation."

I walked to the window and took in several deep breaths.

"No one wins, June. Money is not a win. Trafficking on lost souls is evil and I don't play that game. Now, you get out. And you tell your pal Walter that I don't rat, even on scumbags like him. But you also tell him if he goes too far and someone really gets hurt, he'll go to prison, by the grace of G-d, where the sex he likes so much will spin his head. Even as a doctor, I have no desire to heal you. Now, I'm taking my session fee from this cash and throwing you out forever. Don't cross my path again." (True enough, I had lost all compassion for this woman, and I could not live with my own negative feelings, even in a transference form, much less hers.)

She stared at me, ready to respond with some vicious retort, but thought better of it and gathered up her money and drugs. At the door she turned back. "OK, Doc, I'm gone. But know this. Winners win and losers can't find their way out of quicksand. You'll be gone within weeks if not months. And, by the way, you're the first man to refuse an offer to fuck me. Hey, maybe you're a homo."

I sat down and caught my breath. It wasn't even eight o'clock and I'd just passed through yet another unexpected ordeal. June's newspaper had fallen beneath the coffee table. To my horror, the headline was: SUICIDE COP HAD JUST LEFT SHRINK'S OFFICE. Underneath was a photo of me looking dazed, handing Officer Stone the gun I had taken from Greenspan. Further down the garbled report was a mention of the fact that I had also killed the husband of a patient the previous month, making me sound like a trigger-happy kook.

I was quoted as having said, "There's normal anxiety and there's heightened anxiety brought on by traumatic events such as the ones Captain Greenspan had recently experienced. He was at war with himself." The statement was vague and lame, but I couldn't very well have said, "You would have all looked down on him anyway for being a big, butch, homosexual cop."

I wanted to go home to shower June's vile scent off my body, but I knew I was where I needed to be. In my chair waiting for my next patient.

# THIRTY

Judy was waiting for me on the stoop in front of the building. She wore a short, lime-green skirt, a yellow linen blouse cinched at the waist with a patent leather belt, and had caught up her mass of light-brown hair in a tortoise shell clip. I was touched by her effort to look pretty for me, but when I told her how pretty she looked, she waved away the compliment. "I still have graham cracker crumbs under my nails."

We walked to a local joint up the street called Lucy's and took a table outside in the warm spring evening. The young waitress came with menus. "Hey there, Judy. White wine?"

I ordered Crown Royal on the rocks. "So I take it you're a regular here."

"Yeah, I've been here on other dates. Sorry, I mean, not that this is a 'date.' We're just having a bite."

"Well, whatever it is, I'm happy to be here with you. Thank you for suggesting it."

The drinks arrived and I held my glass up for a toast. "To whatever this moment might be called." I then tossed back way too big a gulp.

Judy took a ladylike sip. "After every breakup, I think I'd be better off forgetting about finding a soulmate. Actually, I love working with the kids, making dinner for my dad, hanging out. But, after a while, I suddenly feel so—I don't know—so abnormal for not wanting more." She sighed. "I guess dating is like riding a bicycle. You just keep getting back on."

"I never learned to ride a bike," I said.

"Well, it's never too late." Our eyes met.

Then, feeling a little self-conscious, we sat in silence and studied the menus as if there would be an exam to follow.

"OK, Elias, what looks good?"

"The super-duper cheeseburger with a side of king-sized onion rings," I replied.

"Heart attack food! I'll have the chicken Caesar."

As the waitress took our order I decided to be reckless and get another round of drinks.

The evening was pleasant and it was good to be sitting outside in the fresh air rather than at home where every room seemed hermetically sealed with the memories trapped inside. And, truth be told, it was nice to sit across from a pretty, sympathetic woman, no matter how surreal it all seemed.

"So, Elias, what happened?"

"With what?"

"With your marriage? It's over, right?"

"A long time ago," I replied.

Smooth jazz wafted from a nearby building.

"You know what I'm going to do?" I finally said. "I'm going to buy myself a Jeep. A two-toned Jeep. The front will be blue and the back red or black . . . or maybe even neon yellow."

"Neon yellow?"

"I'm done with conservative colors."

"Why a jeep?"

"I'll put a plow on it so I can get around when it snows upstate."

She laughed. "Well, the deer will definitely see you coming!"

"Do you like jeeps?" I asked.

The food arrived and the waitress slammed it on the table unceremoniously. "Enjoy!" she said cheerily as she sped off.

"Elias, you're so . . . Well, I'm just someone observing from afar . . ."

"I'm so what?" She was not a Grace in terms of intellect, but she was earnest and instinctive.

She seemed flustered at her own boldness. "I don't know . . . alluring? Smart! I mean, you're a genius. You're wise and funny. And Elias, in a non-movie star way, you're really handsome."

A young happy couple passed by giggling, holding hands. They paused to nuzzle and then moved on, madly in love for sure. A wave of jealousy arose within me.

"You know, every time I see kids in love like that, I think, 'How long will that last? How ugly will it all be when their love ends?'" My cynicism caught both of us by surprise.

"So we shouldn't be allowed to have fun along the way? I mean, why not?" she said. "Isn't there more to life than the problems you hear about in your office every day?"

"I'm not so sure," I answered quietly.

"But at least you're always helping people, right?"

"I emotionally abandoned my wife and my sons years ago so I could spend more time with strangers trying to 'fix them' as if I fancy myself some sort of mechanic for the human race. I'm not sure I see the point anymore."

"Don't say that. You can't give up what you do."

"Why? What keeps you going?"

"Hope," she replied.

"And how is that working out?"

"Well, I'm here with you. So I would have to say well." She smiled and touched my hand. Reflexively, I pulled it back. She flushed.

"I'm sorry, Judy." Suddenly I felt incredibly vulnerable. "I don't know how to respond anymore. I mean, other than Grace all these years, women who talk to me are patients and they're off limits. Your alluring genius of a shrink is at sea. I feel somewhat confused and guilty . . ."

"Guilty?"

"That Grace just left, that I'm out with you . . ."

"Elias, Grace had many—"

The waitress came by with our second round of drinks and looked at our untouched plates. "Something wrong with the food?"

I bit into my burger, nodded—"Mmmmm . . ."—and she moved away, satisfied.

Yes, of course I knew Grace had had other guys besides the ape-man, but I had convinced myself it was just an awful phase. She would fulfill her need to be free and it would end. We would be Elias and Grace again. How stupid. I made some headway into my second drink, knowing what Judy was about to say. I didn't want to hear the words but didn't stop her from saying them.

Judy was looking at me intently. "I mean, you guys had an open marriage, right? That's what she told my dad when he came in to unplug the sink one afternoon. He didn't think anyone was home. I mean, it was awkward but . . . you knew, right?"

Suddenly, I couldn't swallow. I willed myself to pick up my water glass and suppressed the urge to cough. I croaked, "There are real marriages and there are also people determined to plow through all sorts of crap to retain the status quo. There's no such thing as a successful 'open marriage.' It's a contradiction in terms." I was beginning to feel light-headed and concentrated on my onion rings. I hadn't eaten much in days.

"Maybe you need a vacation, Elias. I mean, all this shock, carrying the woe of the world. We all have to realize that it's possible to break and fall to the ground like a broken horse."

"I'm more of an ant."

She looked puzzled.

"An ant can carry almost a thousand times its body weight. Think about that. An ant can live without air for days or under water for more than a week. It can survive without its head for days, still performing its chores for the colony even while in distress."

"Without a head!"

"Absolutely!"

The image was ridiculous. She began to laugh and it was contagious. Laughter poured out of me like water out of a faucet. The release button had been hit, and my laughter redoubled hers. Several people looked over, curious. When one of us got it under control, the other would lose it. Finally, we were wiping away tears, struggling to catch our collective breath.

"Oh, my G-d! I'll never step on another ant as long as I live," said my new ally.

Like truth serum, the alcohol coursed through me. "You're one smart, funny, compassionate woman, Judy. I'm so happy to have taken you out on this non-date." I heard myself slur a little.

Judy signaled for the check. "Come on, we're both exhausted. I have to be ready for the patter of little feet at seven thirty. And I'm sure you need to gird your loins for your patients, right?"

I loved the way she added "right?" without expecting an answer. She handed her waitress friend cash while I was still fumbling for my wallet.

Walking home, I could think of nothing but falling into orange and yellow sheets. I swayed a little and Judy took my arm. "I usually don't drink so much," I said. She laughed and above us a moon appeared.

At the building, she gave me a hug and climbed the stoop to her door. "Sweet dreams!" she called down. That was it. She didn't ask for anything, didn't press me to come in. Her life was complete with or without a man.

As I fell asleep, I had a flash of June, lying there spread open like a bear trap, ready to take, to do damage. And then there was this relatively plain woman living right upstairs who had been invisible to me all along, making me laugh as I had not laughed in years. Seeing me home, insisting that I go to sleep. She was like the sister I had never had.

Sweet dreams.

# THIRTY-ONE

I had teenage butterflies by the time I got to work. After decades of monogamy, I had actually been out on a date, or sort of a date! Taking the advice I had recently given Susan Decker, I went next door to get a glazed donut for its "calming influence." I also picked up the morning paper, which featured page after page of rehash on the death of Captain Greenspan: photos of him graduating the police academy, photos of him shaking the mayor's hand after the bank robbery. My name was mentioned but it seemed that the shrink-suicide angle was fading.

I returned to the office and finished my coffee as I scanned through my notes on my upcoming appointments and perused the mail. A letter with a Boston return address caught my attention. It was from the Beantown Police Department, from a Detective Rogers. He informed me he would be in New York over the coming months and wanted to stop by and discuss a case that concerned someone he believed was my patient. I was puzzled as to who it might be; I would, of course, be as helpful as my professional doctor-patient confidentiality would allow.

Then I focused on Rebecca's file. The last time we spoke, which was days ago, I had scolded her for being reckless. And yes, that *was* my place. Her choices were her own but, considering the life and abuse she had endured, I felt strongly that it was my professional right to caution her. When she and Danny arrived at nine I was prepared to broach this concern and see where it led. I was in no mood for risks either for my patients or the advice and treatment I would offer.

Rebecca looked radiant, young and happy, almost girlish. She was dressed in a conservative navy business suit, with shoes to match. She wore little makeup and her hair was pulled back into a tight bun, revealing small pearl earrings.

Danny was majestic. I recalled him as a man of size, but he seemed more than that. Regal and elegant, he wore the Hassidic long black coat and hat, giving him gravitas. Unlike the first meeting, he was relaxed, calm and still clearly enamored with Rebecca. He offered his trademark dead-fish handshake with a slight bow, and I motioned for him to take a seat next to Rebecca, who sat beaming on the couch.

Unexpectedly, my heart swelled with pride. This woman had been through more hell and misery than most anyone could survive and yet here she sat, wearing a smile that would light a moonless night. I was well aware of the human spirit and how it often overcame distress. The clock had ticked forward for Rebecca and misery had lost its grip on her. I was filled with a renewed vigor to give her the best of my best.

Rebecca began immediately. "Doctor, when last we spoke you were clearly disapproving of me. You said I was reckless and fragile. And that I could find myself back in hell if I were not careful." Danny held her hand and his head nodded his acquiescence.

"Rebecca, I was not disapproving. I was reminding you of what you've been through and that you do remain fragile. I was asking you to reflect on your actions and to think. With no disrespect to Danny—I don't know him—I have questions regarding his intentions and how they will affect you."

"And what are those questions?" she asked, suddenly defensive.

"Simply, you and I have discussed a different future for you. A life that gives you wealth and fulfillment without compromising your self-respect. Yet you bring this man to meet me and refer to him as your 'sponsor,' although he has a traditional Jewish marriage. And yet, what has he done to better your life? What will he do in the future to better your life?"

"He loves me, he doesn't judge me and he will help me make more money faster than before so I can live my dreams." She sounded fifteen. Danny continued to hold her hand, nodding rhythmically.

"Rebecca, I make no judgments either. You've climbed out of oblivion and now can find a road to a healthy life, one that's filled with caring and even love. But I don't see that happening with the course of action that you and Danny have undertaken. Enhancing your breasts to charge more money, mirrored rooms to increase fees? Do what you want, but I don't believe it's a safe path to what you really want."

They were both listening intently.

"In my opinion, Danny should want you out of your former life, not after more money is earned but now; yesterday in fact. That is a real expression of love and concern. Only then can you work with me on plotting a healthy future."

Upon hearing those words Danny stood up, towering over me. I felt like a Lilliputian.

"Doctor, you don't trust me, nu?"

"I'm not saying that," I answered, uncertain whether I should bolt.

"Do you believe in courage, Doctor?"

"Yes."

"Deep courage, when you think you might never take in another breath?"

"I most certainly do."

"Enough so that you know how special or how rare it is in a person?"

He had my attention. Although I had to strain to understand his words through his thick accent, I caught the gist.

"I love this *tatala* because she has courage, so deep she does not know of it. I love her 'cause she smiles at what is bitter and believes the next day will bring good news and a blessing. And she trusts you, which shows that she is wise. You know that I tested you the other day with cash? I put on a little show to see what you would do? And you did right! 'No!' you said, 'cash is wrong!' And then you wonder if I am good for this woman because you love her and want good."

I had to interrupt. "She's my patient, and that's why I show concern, not because I love her. Care, yes. But love is an emotion I must hold at bay to help my patients."

"Motives, yes, motives is good." He turned to Rebecca and she nodded in agreement. "And you are right today, Dr. Elias. I should not allow her to spend another second on her back, not a one. And that story about the mirrors was also a test." Now Rebecca seemed surprised. "Maybe wrong of me, but perhaps you will understand if I tell you a story. Nu?"

"The floor is yours," I replied.

He began to pace slowly, gathering his thoughts.

"When Hitler attacked Poland in 1939 I was twelve-year-old. The fears of death by the Nazis filled one's heart and there was little sleep as we all felt that death was a single breath away.

The Germans had tanks and airplanes and mortars and so many soldiers! They covered the land like weeds. You could hear them miles away as their boots hit the ground, promising a merciless end. The land was parched and they came through our villages to burn our homes, kill our children and rape our women. We fought. We had courage.

"But we fought with blades and our soldiers rode on horses and not in jeeps or carried by tanks like them. My home, Bialystok, was one of the first villages to see such godless massacre. The Germans surrounded our village and shot anyone that moved—women, children, old peoples. The ground was red with blood. We had a village of almost twenty thousand and within minutes they were lined up and shot with machine guns. The Germans took whatever had a value from the dead bodies and then pushed the lost souls into an open mass grave for the vultures that began to circle before the death was even over.

"I was twelve and somehow me and thirteen other boys fled to the woods and hid for days as the Germans marched further into our homeland, thinking they had left only the dead behind."

He paused and took a handkerchief from his coat pocket and wiped tears off his cheeks. He sat and took a long drink of water and blinked as if he wanted to see the memory clearly so he could tell the tale with belief, despite the fact that it was unbelievable.

"If you intend to kill a people then make sure you finish, for revenge is a powerful voice that never falls silent. My friends who had run to safety found each other over the next few days. As the Germans marched on, we found places we might hide and not be discovered. We ate berries and rabbit and horses that had been slayed and left behind for the vermin. We had no guns, although some of us had knives or had recovered swords from fallen brethren.

"We had no future. But we had courage and we had hope and we had hate. So much hate in our hearts it could move mountains. And we had G-d! And so, even though it sounded like a child's war game, we banded together and called ourselves the 'Bialystok Resistance' and we pledge to one another to seek our freedom, pray to our G-d and destroy the Nazis.

"I became a 'captain' of boys my own age who had found a way to escape. We raided Nazi camps at night, killed them like the animals they were, stole their guns and food and left them for rats to feed on. We became old before we had a chance to be young boys who played games, yet we became stronger. In each village we found a few survivors to join with us and we grew in numbers and became a dangerous enemy. The Nazis couldn't find us as we moved at night and hid during day. While they looked to wipe out thousands, we prayed to save a few.

"By the time I was fifteen I had killed men with my knife, slit their throats for blankets or rations to feed my shrunken belly. And the resistance followed me and my mission.

"The months, they passed. Death was always with us, sleep never peaceful and fear always sat on the shoulder. But we remained strong, and as the days passed the Nazis began to lose ground in Poland and throughout Europe, and the tide of their tyranny began to lose its grip. We made raids on the camps and saved some of our brothers and discovered that the Nazis ran with fear when they were faced with the ferocity of our vengeance.

"Then, in 1945, the allies were about to free the camps and try the Nazis for their crimes. Try them? Give them the chance to defend what they had done. They had covered our homeland, our villages and our people in blood and death. To even think they deserved a second chance or a chance at an explanation was unthinkable.

"So we raided the homes of the commandants who had tortured the Jews, gassed us till death. And when we raided the homes of German officers we saw the way they lived, golden on the deaths of the Jew. We killed them without mercy and took back the spoils they had taken from us, along with dignity and life. We found diamonds and gold and jewelry, became marauders, and stole back what was stolen. Then, when the allies arrived to free our brothers and sisters, we hid again. This time to keep the wealth we had taken back. I was a twenty-year-old boy who had become old all too soon.

"We did not go to Israel because we believe in the Messiah and not in Zionism. At great cost, we traveled to America and built communities surrounded by invisible walls to protect us against further humiliation and offense. And we survived! In fact, we more than survived. We built synagogues and prayed without the threat of death. We took *our* spoils of war and we built businesses while the Americans looked at our *zitzuz* and piety and garb and thought us the freak. But we prospered and many of us became rich. Does money give back life? No! A man is a man and money is simply a way to give back choices we once had that were stolen from us. And in America money is G-d more than the one we pray to.

"So for years I lived with pain and memories of horrors that those who walk the streets of gold here in NY will never imagine. They look at me in my clothes that honor my history and think me a monkey in the zoo. And my hate kept growing, staining my heart even though I had a wife and a good life.

"And then I meet Rebecca. And, yes, she is beautiful. But she also listens to my sadness and doesn't judge me for the way I dress or the beard I wear. She shows compassion. Compassion, a word I thought was gone forever. And she says I can have her body, find pleasure in her breast and the feeling of her soft skin. My G-d, my prayers have been answered.

"Do I think what my *tatala* has been doing is good? No. Do I know *her* secrets? I think so. She has told me of her horrors and yet, as with the things I did to survive, she also did what she had to do. No matter what my G-d thinks of me and my Rebecca and the things we were forced to do, he must understand that the killing I did was what needed to be done. I spend every night without sleep thinking the young men, boys like me, were the sons of mothers who will cry the rest of their days because of me. Evil leads to more evil."

He stopped pacing and again wiped away his tears and perspiration. Then he sat across from me and took my hands in his. "Dr. Elias," he said with great intensity, "I must ask you for a promise to me."

I remained silent and looked back into his dark eyes.

"You must promise to protect Rebecca. To make sure she treats herself with respect that she never was given. I need this pledge from you, a man of ethics and heart and compassion, so I can do what I am about to do and never doubt myself. Do you give me your word to be there for her? For me?"

I took a long time to answer. "Danny, as long as Rebecca is my patient I promise I'll be here for her and do what you ask. If and when she's truly well and no longer a patient I will still honor your request."

And then we sat in silence, not knowing what Danny was going to do. Our wondering filled the room.

Finally, he stood up again and bent down to kiss Rebecca sweetly on her forehead, the way a parent kisses a child before sleep. He then reached into the inside pocket of his coat and removed a business-sized envelope and handed it to Rebecca.

"Open," he said quietly.

She did. Her eyes darted from Danny's to mine to the paper she had removed from the envelope. Her hands shook and she began to cry. "Oh my, oh my," she cried. "Elias, what is this?"

She passed me the document. It was a certified check payable to Rebecca for five million dollars. Tears streamed down Danny's face. I have to confess, I could barely speak. "Well, Rebecca, it appears to be your future and the end of a dark past."

"Something good! Finally something good!" He opened his arms and she embraced him with all her might.

"Thank you, thank you," she said a million times and, with each thank you, her frightening past faded away. It was a glorious moment and nothing else mattered.

## THIRTY-TWO

Having been in practice for decades I had learned that wishes seldom, if ever, come true. Life is about reality. More often a harsh one in which the heart breaks and healing comes at a price. Yet this morning I had witnessed wish fulfillment to such an amazing degree that I made a conscious decision to start believing again in possibility. Perhaps even I might fall in love again, win the lottery or find some sustained new joy in the madness and the chaos that filled my days.

I'd begin by smiling more often, peeling away layers of cynicism, and if a genie showed up for a session, I wouldn't actually charge him currency, but ask for three wishes in exchange. I wanted to have at least one moment that matched the magic in the room when Danny fitted Rebecca with her glass slipper, a perfect fit that was long overdue.

Next, I wanted to see what others saw in me. Women told me that I was attractive, that my eyes were wise and kind. If I could learn to see that in myself, I might find my way back to Elias, "just Elias" of old—not the aging, discouraged doctor who struggled through each difficult day alone. I had often thought to myself, "Thank G-d I'm not a trauma surgeon whose decisions could end a life." But, as it turned out, a bad decision on my part had ended a life. I never should have let the captain leave my office. I needed to get past that.

The third wish? Maybe I would use it tonight. Perhaps my session with the beautiful, emerging personality of Susan Decker would be a bridge to a real relationship. I would eventually get her a new therapist so there would be no conflict of interest, and she would become the incredibly wonderful, worthy mate of my future. With renewed hope, I continued through my day with an inner smile, saw patients both old and new. I remained focused, listened, reflected and gave away a little piece of myself to each of them. At last it was Thursday and my clocks told me that the day was done.

I had brought a change of clothes to work, and dressed quickly into a taupe linen suit over a cotton, open-neck dress shirt and two-toned wing tips that put a skip in my step. As I closed the door on my office my heart started to beat a bit too fast, my palms became sweaty and my face flushed. Now that my day was complete and I was actually on my way to meet Susan Decker, I felt like a high school kid about to go to his first prom.

As I hailed a cab, I gave myself a stern talking to. This was *not* a date, I said to myself, as I had already cautioned her in no uncertain terms. This was an after-hours session arranged to accommodate her needs. I rode across town, reviewing her case, gratified that she had come so far in such a relatively short time. Still, Susan was vulnerable and in need of a long course of therapy. She was most definitely off limits, at least for now.

I had selected a small Spanish restaurant on the corner of Charles and West 10th Street in the heart of the Village. My taxi pulled up to the front of Sevilla, having traveled over old cobblestone streets lit by the converted gas lamps of early New York. The night was warm with a light breeze . . . magical. I paid the driver and stood outside for a few moments, listening to the sounds of the city. Ambient, indecipherable banter and laughter from the open cafes in the neighborhood filled the evening air, along with the scents of the Spanish delicacies wafting from the restaurant kitchen.

The setting was more romantic than I had remembered, more than I had ever noticed. Small, cozy booths glowing with candlelight lined the windowed bar area, inviting intimacy. Each table boasted a perfect red rose in a bud vase. One young couple sipped margaritas and stared into each other's eyes. An older married couple toasted with Sangria.

I realized my folly at once. Without conscious intention, I had set a trap! This was not a setting for a therapy session. I was setting the stage for my own inappropriate fantasy to play out. Briefly, I considered leaving, phoning with an excuse. But I couldn't bear the thought of being a coward. I perched on a bar stool and rehearsed how the session would start, how I would build a wall with my professional demeanor and dispel any thoughts of intimacy.

But no sooner had the bartender approached to take my order than I heard my name called from down the room. Susan stepped from the booth tucked away in the far corner, looking stunning in a black low-cut cocktail dress that stopped well above the knee. She smiled—dazzling—her face framed by some sort of softer hairstyle. I took another mental ice-water shower and waved casually, forced myself to walk slowly toward her, and put out my hand just as I sensed she was moving in to hug me.

"Didn't see you!" I said, cheerily pumping her hand. I slid into the booth across from her and looked out into the spring night.

"Elias, thank you so much for this meeting. You're a lifesaver. Knowing I would see you tonight gave me peace of mind and I'm so grateful. And this place is so lovely. It's like being in Spain without the jet lag!"

I was more uncomfortable than ever and I became suddenly perky and out of breath. "Yes, quite true. Yes, it is a nice spot. I've been here off and on over the years. Why don't we take a quick look at the menu and order before the place gets too noisy?"

She took her menu and leaned over so I knew what was available under her dress inside her scanty black lace brassiere. "Why the rush, Elias? Let's have a glass of wine and get settled. Hear about your day. Get to know one another a bit."

"Actually, not a good idea," I replied. "We should both be clear headed for your therapy session. Actually, now that we're here, I regret having selected this place. Forgive me." I gestured for the waiter.

"OK, but it's a special session and I bought this dress especially for tonight." She smiled and I steeled myself to withstand her warmth.

"Although your outfit and your looks are both fetching, we're here because I extended my hours tonight so you would have a companion, and not consider going to 'the club.' No flirting allowed!" I was trying for casual humor but it was awful. I sounded like an old school marm shaking her finger.

"Well, a glass of wine would do wonders for you, mister. You have issues that I believe might even match mine. So let's relax a bit first."

"My issues are not on the docket tonight, Susan. I am, at least for the moment, your therapist and nothing more." And how badly I was wanting more!

She was taken aback.

The waiter came over. "Are you ready to order?"

I responded curtly, "Give us another minute, please." Puzzled, he walked away.

Here it was. The moment that defines your character, your ethics and integrity. Trying to do the right thing while nursing a broken heart; mind in terrible conflict with two diametrically opposed debaters talking at once. "Screw the therapy. You've wanted Susan Decker from the first moment she walked into your office!" "Doctors don't act on their 'wants' with sick patients!" "She's coming out on the other side of her obsessions. This is the kind, warm, caring person that you have been longing for your whole life!" "No! Not possible!"

Susan jumped back in. "Elias, knowing I was going to see you tonight . . . I want you to know that I never thought about the club. I wanted to be with you. I'm embarrassed to say this, but I know you want me to be honest. Well, I fantasized that I would become your . . . special friend, and we'd talk about other things and you'd walk me home—"

I cut her off. "I'm truly flattered, Susan. But I'm your doctor and no more. I'll find you another therapist, most likely a woman. I'm not here to fulfill a fantasy and replace one dysfunctional behavior with another. I've practiced for over thirty years and never crossed the line. To do so would shatter the foundation of my work. I promised you dinner so stay and enjoy, my treat, but keep away from 'the club,' as that is what we both want. I'll phone you tomorrow with a suggestion as to who might replace me."

"Shatter the foundation of your work?" She looked as sad and confused as I felt—a know-it-all doctor spewing rhetoric while denying his own feelings.

I put money on the table for her dinner and got up to leave with a pit in my stomach. "Susan, there's something interfering with my ability to be effective this evening. To my great regret I simply can't continue."

I offered my hand in goodbye, which she refused to take.

"Good luck," I said and left.

I lingered outside the restaurant. Schmuck that I was, I was not going to be one of the many in my line of work who took advantage of a patient, broke the law or put my needs above my oath. It took all my self-control not to go back inside and take that hurt young woman in my arms. To find solace for both of us at least for a night. Yet it would create emotional carnage, and I was not lonely enough for that. I remained outside for a very long time.

Staring at my reflection in the glass door, my heart sank. *That can't be* me, I thought, a "sad sack," slumped over, wearing a frown and the burdens of disappointment. After all those frantic hours burning the midnight oil, the college degrees, the early mornings conscientiously preparing for each patient, I was just a middle-aged doctor with new streaks of gray hair defining me. A horny, middle-aged doctor. I had been the head of the class, the hardest worker, the star, the innovator. Where were the accolades now?

Impulsively, I re-entered the restaurant and rushed down to the booth in the corner. Susan was staring into a glass of white wine. Startled, she raised her head. "Please let me do the talking, Susan. You do look terrific. You look fucking gorgeous and I long for you, as any healthy man would. But here's the good news. There's someone out there who will commit to you totally, to the woman you are becoming. And I'm one wounded son of a bitch. Within the past week, a client committed suicide and my wife left me—"

"Oh, I'm so sorry—"

"No, I'm sorry!" I had to finish. "I came here wanting intimacy as badly as you do. But what I must not do is betray your trust."

Her eyes welled up with tears.

"And you're right, Susan, I do need help. I do have issues, but you can't let that complicate your journey right now. As promised, I'll call with the number of someone who will complete our work. You deserve a good life, Susan. Forgive me, I have to leave you!"

As I bolted, I took with me a precious snapshot, the split second when her glorious, beatific smile of forgiveness beamed through her tears. She had given me, in essence, my release.

I walked for a long time. It was I who desperately needed therapy. I could see it so clearly now. Caught in the quicksand of others' problems, I had left my needs behind. I was always urging my patients to work on their issues, to explore their thoughts, consider options. "You have to be willing to do the hard work," I had often said. But I had never been willing to do the hard work on myself. I was too busy. I was the classic example of the adage "don't do as I do, do as I say." Physician, heal thyself!

For much of my life I had felt complete, traveling down the "yellow brick road" as a man of import and accomplishment, knowing, without a doubt, that I mattered. I was making a difference, leaving my mark. I had a lovely home and a brilliant wife who supported me fully. The fiction of that life imploded the day Grace asked for us to "talk." At least that was the day I acknowledged the myth of our relationship.

By the time I got to Washington Square Park, I was awash in self-pity. Why can't I find a partner outside this awful circle of my profession? A kind, healthy woman who will get that I am complex and help me work things out, will think me funny and handsome, who will look forward to seeing me at the end of her work day and be happy to wake in my arms each morning. One who will give me long, lingering kisses, softly, so that my burdens fade away. Someone who is smart, not afraid to take me on, but doesn't need to compete with me.

I stopped in my tracks. There was such a person. She would probably still be sitting on the stoop with her day-care kids, waiting for their parents who were rushing from work to pick them up. She would be brushing cracker crumbs off their clothes. Unlike Grace, she wasn't particularly attractive or sexy, but she was someone who had won my heart when she had said, "Sweet dreams." Rather than ask for more of my time and attention for herself, she knew that I needed to rest. She cared about what I needed! My anxiety waned and I quickened my step. I was about to use my third wish on the proverbial girl next door.

## THIRTY-THREE

It was a Friday in late May and, after weeks of false spring, the weather was perfect. My last appointment had canceled, so I sat in a small outdoor cafe nursing an iced tea and people watching as the workday came to an end. I had brought my new mutt, Titus, with me to work and now he sat quietly at my feet, studying the four-legged denizens of lower New York City who trotted by.

I heard my name called from across the street. "Elias? Elias Meyers, is that you?"

It was Susan Decker, dodging traffic and racing toward my table. I hadn't seen or heard from her since that night when I walked out on her at the Seville many years earlier. I stood up to greet her as she approached and offered my hand in welcome. She ignored the gesture and hugged me close as if I had just come home from a long journey.

"Elias, Elias Meyers, my very own soothsayer. You look wonderful! Younger, more fit—you must be spending time at the gym."

I smiled weakly. "It must be the gardening, I guess, and the long walks with Titus here. Spending less time in the city, smelling the roses a bit."

She got down on a knee and petted Titus vigorously. "What is he, part Lab?" Susan looked radiant, calmer, less pinched, relaxed and happy.

"That's what they thought at the shelter." Titus gave her an ear kiss and resumed his dog-watching.

"What are you doing here?" she asked, sitting opposite me.

"My office, same place just a couple of blocks away. What brings you downtown?"

She beamed and the sun seemed to shine brighter.

"That therapist you recommended, Barbara Klein, she moved her office down here recently. I've been seeing her regularly for over 10 years now, except in August when all of you go to Shrink Islands to rest up for a new year of crazies."

I laughed. "They aren't actually 'islands.' Shrinks gravitate to places like Provincetown or Cape May."

"I see." She smiled. "So I couldn't help but notice, you're wearing a wedding ring. Who's the lucky girl?"

"She's the head of social services up in Katonah where we live. And you—married?"

She flashed an engagement ring. "June tenth!" she squealed, like a gushing high school cheerleader. "I can't believe it, but I'm ready. I'm healthy and happy."

"That's good, Susan, that's really good." I found that my eyes welled with tears. "I'm glad for you."

She hit me affectionately on the shoulder the way I had seen women do to their husbands or boyfriends when they had said something amusing or affectionate.

"Me too, me too, Elias. I'm very hopeful."

And then we were silent. Strangers whose paths had crossed a long time ago.

"Are you still with your law firm?" I asked, just to ask something.

"No, I sold my partnership and moved out of the city two years ago. I live in a small town upstate called Canajoharie. I have a few clients and I'm the local DA. Simple and fulfilling." And then she looked at me, waiting for something more.

"Well, small world. Canajoharie is just a few miles from my house in Katonah."

"Get out! So what do you do when you're up there?"

"I've split my practice between Manhattan and Balboa, where I can see patients for way smaller fees. And I've also become somewhat of an accidental farmer—a Jew with a green thumb!"

She laughed. "You? No way!"

"It's true! This year, I planted a field of alfalfa and another field of cauliflower and I have one whole acre dedicated to organic sweet corn. I play the saxophone in the fields and I'm accompanied by Titus here who howls along."

She laughed. "You know, Elias," she said, "I'm no longer your patient and you still owe me the pleasure of your company at a real dinner. I'm not a bad cook. The four of us could do a barbeque."

"That's true. We all have to eat."

She handed me her card. "Well, until then! Great seeing you. Can't keep a therapist waiting!"

And she was off.

It had been a year of closure for me. Right before Thanksgiving I was at a convention at Harvard when I overheard two colleagues talking about Dr. Brennan being arrested for being a major drug dealer. His cohort, June, had also been arrested on drug charges, prostitution, and grand larceny. Along with "massive neuron brain shifts and the results when different receptors are reached," it was the buzz of the Harvard Convention. I realized how many of us had known about Brennan before he was arrested, including me. *Shame on all of us*, I thought. It had taken the overdose of a young woman to tip off the authorities. Ah, justice.

Then, one day in early January, the street buzzer rang as I was putting my files away for the day. I checked the monitor and found to my delight that it was Jimmy standing in the freezing cold. I hadn't spoken to him in years. He bounded up the stairs with energy and we greeted each other warmly. His gaze was steady, he had gained weight, and he seemed an inch or two taller.

"Dr. Elias, I painted this especially for you," he said, presenting me with one of his latest works—it was an abstract watercolor of a deep-blue gentle ocean with the frigate, *Constitution*, sailing with the American Flag of thirteen colonies, and the "Don't Tread on Me" below it, beautifully framed. "I wanted you to have this as a thank you."

He told me that his mother had met a man and married, and she and her new husband had a small gallery together in Troy, New York, where Jimmy sold his work. As it turned out, his mom's suicide attempt had landed her in Kings County Hospital G Building, staffed with clinical social workers, psychiatrists, and psychiatric nurses, thanks to a generous federal grant. She was back on her feet and Jimmy was on his way to meet a female colleague for a drink. When he left, I took down my diplomas and hung his painting over my desk. It was a much more important testament to my work.

In April I had received a tearful call from Rebecca. Her great mentor, Danny, had passed away at home peacefully, with his wife by his side. She asked me to accompany her to his funeral and act as a couple so that Rebecca would not stand out. Danny's wife didn't know of her and she'd be one of the few non-Hasidim to be attending that funeral. I agreed to do it even though it was short notice and I'd have to cancel some patients. Rebecca had come a long way and genuinely grieved over the loss of Danny, who had started her on the road to real estate development and philanthropy. The Upper Westside Women's shelter now bore a plaque with her name.

It had been almost two years since I had testified at the trial that helped put two of Rebecca's attackers in a maximum-security prison for life. The other two had died in a shootout with the police while they were attacking another woman. Detective Tom Rogers, the one who had spoken kindly to her in the hospital years before, had finally connected the ringleader's lost wallet to her case and had been on their trail since Rebecca's attack a lifetime ago.

As I sat there, mulling over the various people and the contacts I'd had, I thought of my parents. Mother always used to say, "When it's cold outside, listen to your mother. Wear a hat, a muffler, and button up your pea coat. When you're sad, just eat a good meal." My father's unfailing wisdom was, "Remember, all you need is a good whore, and that will take care of all of your problems." Would that it were that simple.

Titus sat up and wagged his tail. Judy pulled up and opened the hatchback. He jumped in, eager for the ride home. I still had to pinch myself every time I saw her. Somehow, propelled by my parent's narrow escape from the Nazis, I had careened forward all my life, racing to find something I could never have defined, something I finally came to believe didn't exist. I had always looked for external signs of status: degrees, money, books published. And here it was, so simple: a rescue dog that howled along with me in the cauliflower field, Jimmy's painting above my desk and this woman, my Judy, who had not one pretentious bone in her body. All those years later, I had finally found my way over a rainbow.

# AFTERWORD
From Dr. Manny Rich

I've practiced for almost fifty-five years, going into my fifty-sixth year shortly. Maybe you could make up stories such as those presented here, but for the people I know who have lived such stories, treatment requires much courage, patience, knowledge, and compassion on the part of the therapist. It is essential that we who practice have therapy for ourselves, even intermittently, so we don't lose our souls along the way, as I almost did. Everyone lives, to a certain extent, with emotional anxieties, physical ailments, and emotional losses. The patients have theirs, and it's our job to tend to theirs while we continue to confront our own.

Even after seventeen years of formal training in social work, integrative behavioral science, psychotherapy and psychoanalysis, mental health consultation, and supervision of the analytic process, I never believed that I knew enough. Subsequently, I joined private study groups to learn more, and after that I met with colleagues regularly so I could further enrich my knowledge. The well is bottomless.

I learned early on that I had an ability to read people instinctively and—whether I felt that I had enough knowledge or not—grasp the essences of their personalities. I realized that I needed both knowledge and instinct to help my patients, along with compassion and understanding. Therapy, after all, is a remedial, educational, medical, psychological, sociological tool. Both knowledge and instinct are essential, as is being a non-judgmental listener. It also pays to breathe regularly!

There are two main problems a person entering this profession must confront. One is that it requires a person to be shut up inside offices, hospitals, and clinics most of one's life. It's easy to fall into the syndrome of seeing the world through the eyes of patients. The second major problem is purely skeletal! Almost all of us who've practiced consistently for a long time have trouble with our backs. (I have ongoing trouble with L1, L2, L3, L4, L5, and S1.) It pays to spend equal time outside the world of the office.

Everyone needs caring, playfulness, and sexual fulfillment (and physical exercise). Without balance, one cannot put one's own emotions into perspective and, if a therapist is not healthy, how can he or she serve a patient? The analyst must learn how much he or she can take, when he or she needs to break off for self-preservation. He or she also needs to know how much the spouse, children and family need. This all has to be juggled if one enters the field of helping other people.

A generic definition of psychotherapy is to relearn, treat, and mend something that is wrong. In the history of treatment for mentally ill patients, the definition of who is ill and how to define that illness has gone through five cycles of the American Psychiatric Association. The initial treatment codes, which attempted to define what is primarily wrong with an individual seeking treatment, have exploded to include multiple explanations of multiple sub-ailments.

Any analyst worth his salt employs standard educational material, the latest research and a careful review of each case, contextualizing each individual's circumstance, gender and age group. Genetic predispositions also have to be taken into account. After that there is need for a meditation of sorts; an interpretation of all the information filtered through the therapist's instincts based on his or her own life experience. This is the analyst's "transference," an empathetic thought process. Then the analyst needs to surmise a patient's rate of repair, with or without the use of medication, and plot a course of action.

Medication is needed in cases that do not respond to other treatment techniques. Medication can hold a patient so they do not crumble while the analyst works to rebuild or repair the brain structure that has gone awry. Therapy is a long-term process. Sadly, insurance companies encourage the shortest possible treatment with heavy emphasis on medications.

Of grave concern not only to my profession but also to our country are the wars we've been fighting over the past decades and their impact on society. Only recently has the establishment recognized PTSD (post-traumatic stress disorder) and its grave consequences. Many of our troops are coming back from overseas in dire need of long-term counseling and it's not available widely enough, even with the addition of outside contractors. People will line up to help pay for a soldier's limb replacement operation, but few are interested in the epidemic of mental illness that curses our country. And yet the men and women most in need often wind up living in poverty and the farthest from help.

We continue to be stunned by those who are famous and "on top" admitting to depression, drug use, taking their own lives. And yet the real front page stories should be about the under-treated population, particularly vets, who succumb to madness and suicide. We must attract top-notch people to the field who are willing to take on the excruciating, long-term commitment to all people in need. We must fund them so there is no watering down of our standards. If we do not, social disaster is inevitable. Mental illness is a disease and it will not go away like the common cold. Heed the advice of someone who is on the front lines and pay attention, America.

# DEFINITIONS, AND CLINICAL SUMMARY OF THE FICTITIOUS CHARACTERS IN THIS NOVEL

## ANALYTIC PSYCHOTHERAPY

The theories associated with analytic and dynamic therapy have their foundations in culture, economics, biology, and environmental and archeological findings. Research in human development, stages of development (Erickson, Mahler, Bowlby, Greenacre, to name a few of the pioneers in the movement. Freud, both Sigmund and his daughter Anna, Reik and Reisch). Thus the roots are biological, which encompasses neurological, developmental growth models of individuals both normal and neurotic, character disorders, thought disorders, and mood disorders. Religious influences, poverty, wealth, and goals of the culture, birth order, and parent's health—all play vital roles in the understanding and treatment of the "mentally ill."

With this understanding, when one enters therapy the therapist or analyst focuses on the major deficits, whether it be anxiety, depression, rage or hostility, caused by the multiple facets of the pressures heaped on the individual. Coming to therapy is usually the last resort to "correct" someone spinning out of effective adulthood. Adolescent therapy, as well as child therapy, helps get the jump on adult pathos.

First, as Freud indicated, "we must understand" before we plunge in to effect positive change. In the twenty-first century we need not only to understand, but also to effect change to relieve suffering and failure, so that someone can best lead their life. Medication can be helpful. Psychiatric and analytic treatment can go hand in hand with close relationships between the professionals. Psychological assessments are invaluable in enforcing the therapist's understanding and treatment. The patient, if able, can review this work with the therapist.

Concepts:

- Unconscious (UCS) those thoughts, events, memories lost to our awareness, and which motivate, guide, and account for current thoughts, feelings and behavior in our present life. In the UCS rests are earliest yearnings, images, needs, drives, all of which is lost to awareness. On top of all of this rests the reality we live

- Conscious (CS) what we are aware of in the current reality of our lives. It includes our current economic condition, how we have fulfilled, or not, our early childhood needs. The CS enables us to remember what we can emotionally sustain and how we lead our lives. The UCS is interwoven with current reality; moreover the UCS leads the way for survival, self-destructiveness, enjoyable life, etc.

- Transference. The patent sees the analyst in all ways as the people of his (her) past and infuses the therapist with them. The patient can then be treated as the therapist unwinds and corrects the perception of reality from history.

- Countertransference. The therapist responds to the distortions, understanding what the patient *had* experienced, has his own reactions monitored, and works to undo the damage in the patient.

- Therapist transference. He has his own history, his own failures of emotion, achievements, and realistic failures and understands how he sees the patient's inner working as well as his own. He attempts to keep the working 'plane' neutral. He is aware of his own intrapsychic workings.
- Resistance. Untold anxiety stirred up against change. Fear of what will be different and unknown.
- Anxiety. "Signal anxiety," a proper anxiety to warn us of danger. Overwhelming anxiety floods our executive functioning and sense of reality. It is the dread of the present and future.
- Clinical depression. Robs us of pleasure, reality testing; can lead to rage, irritability, weight gain, extreme criticism of self and others. Reality or experiential depression related to every day occurrences. It is the disaster of the past, which cannot be assimilated or diffused. It weighs us down, taking all pleasure from life. It leaves a constant sour taste in our mouths.
- Rage. Misuses aggressive drive, and counters depression intrapsychically. Can keep one together at the price of others (sadism, brutality, insensitivity to others and self).

There are many other terms understood by analysts (interchangeable with therapists) i.e. repression, suppression, denial, intellectualization, minimization, projection as listed below. Definitions are beyond this work.

## DEFENSES

There are many intrapsychic ways to ward off excessive anxiety, rage, depression, etc. Some of these are more harmful for adults, although aid in childhood and adolescence. Defenses serve as a way not to be overwhelmed by internal as well as external forces. I will list only a few: repression, suppression, denial, intellectualization, minimization, illness, headaches, lack of energy, laziness, food, sex addiction, alcohol addiction, drug addiction, greed, hoarding.

You make a list of ways you soothe yourself, avoid, project your feelings onto others, attempt or succeed in controlling others. The list goes on. I have mentioned just a few salient ones.

Treatment can be seen as having four phases, not distinct and ordered, but available through free association; that is, people say whatever comes to mind, and the therapist finds the underlying unconscious theme, a difficult and essential part of "good" therapy. One does not shoot from the hip unless you have lots of practice. The assumption is that you have integrated knowledge, intuition, and experience. Shooting from the hip can be defended with knowledge and experience of self and others.

- Identify the issues.
- Clarify the issues, educate, clear distortions of fact when you can (timing essential, for the patient has "to take in," to absorb, to integrate, to make it his own in his psychic structure. It is

not an outside thought.)
- Interpret the unconscious, make connections for the patient or have the patient make them and you reinforce them.
- Confront—when appropriate, do not allow the patient to escape what he now knows. Ensure he understands the difference between what he knows now and what he believed before.
- Be aware that these four are not so delineated in practice. The practitioner follows, weaves, and threads as the patient free-associates. It is the art integrated with knowledge and experience.

## FREE ASSOCIATION
Mentioned above. All thoughts and feelings or lack thereof count! This is the best way into the unconscious. In analytic treatment CURIOSITY DOES NOT KILL THE CAT. IT IS BEST TO BE CAUTIOUS, SPEAK SOFTLY AND CARRY A LARGE STICK.

I must also warn that in decompensated individuals you want to close the unconscious so that they can function, not be overwhelmed, and then start the reverse process while controlling and building the psychic structures (ego, id, superego. Watch out for the drives for aggression and libido).

## VIGNETTES
For each of the major characters, a short understanding and techniques are discussed as they are presented in the story. Most often self-esteem and self-compassion are distorted, warped, and too critical of self and goals. Lack of self-worth

ends in a person's not being compassionate or forgiving to themselves for flaws, failures, partial successes.

It's important to meld aggression with libido so that love, lust, compassion, passion, a positive energy force is created, fostered, strengthened, so the individual can go forth into the wilderness and do much more than survive.

I hate to say this—it all depends on *trust,* usually developed between the mother and the child within the first six months of life. Mother and father then nurture it until the school years. *Hopefully teachers strengthen this bond.* Schools are the only cultural public institution to affect all individuals. School personnel can correct emotions, strengthen creativity if the parents have not. School's main purpose is to educate, and also to emotionally nurture the next generation. Moreover, extreme deprivation in early childhood (before four years of age) can blunt the effects of schooling.

The greater the disturbance in an individual who seeks treatment, the more parameters may need to be used by the therapist. These can take many forms and are beyond the four principles outlined above.

## REBECCA

Primitive and sophisticated. Brutalized by observance, scant mothering; men are users, brutal and fleeting. There's no warmth in her history. She searches for maternal care anywhere and does not believe it available. Men are "johns" to be pleased, to be used and to take money from for services rendered. She learned to be a sex worker. She had not much self-esteem. She regressed, took heroin and crack, and gradually descended into a nomad's life: living on her wit and her body.

She had to have a *strong mind, with much constitutional energy.* Prison was her salvation. Some professionals saw that. Danny saw that, and she pleased him. He was a soft man with her, a positive male figure.

Other prostitutes whom I treated referred her to me. When she said she didn't want to be a mentally healthy secretary and she had greater financial goals, with also wanting to influence and have a presence in the community, I took note. I understood her quest, her pain, her wish to present a good and powerful image, and I agreed to her terms if she stayed the course in treatment. Funny thing is that I didn't yearn for her sexually. I think I had too much regard for Rebecca's struggles, none of which involved sex.

I used our honest relationship, accurate fact giving, and education, taught normal expectations, taught emotions. With Danny in the picture (a good thing for them both) my own transference and countertransference got in the way. Rebecca steered me correctly so we could continue in our work together. I was then able to review my feelings about their relationship and save the work history we had.

Silence is an important tool. It allows patients to free associate, to think and experience emotions in the safety of the consulting room. It is a place which offers safety, privacy, almost free of judgment, and a place to examine yearnings, wishes, hostilities, rage, despair—the analyst has to be up to the task of understanding, intervening where it does the most good.

## JIMMY

Whatever the pathology before his father's untimely death, he was attached to his mother like glue. His father stood in his way, a good and just Oedipal figure. Did he kill his father to have his mother? In Oedipus, the son blinds himself on his mother's brass nipples, part of her breastplate. That taught him a lesson for "knowing" his mother (in the Biblical sense). But what of his mother, who desperately needed him as a man, and who controlled him as a young boy. She was attractive in her own right—did not she think another man might want her? Was she so shocked and regressed as to hide with her son, who gave to her while she ministered to him?

I actively intervened. I am an authority. I needed to break this up and help Jimmy put himself together. I needed another professional for his mother who would isolate, guilt ridden and perhaps suicidal. I could not see them both. I was the father to the son, as well as the authority and superego to the mother. I acted to support her ego and ego ideal appropriately. Remember the adage "where Id is, let Ego be" (Freud).

The hysterical blindness abated; separation with a positive libido strengthened. There will always be a residue in Jimmy and his mother. Neither Cathy, nor I, nor any other analyst can repair this one hundred per cent.

# ETHAN (ET)

Ethan, a pleasant, typical "garmento" con artist (psychopathic traits, compulsive traits, some remorse, repressive features, to name a few clinical aspects) had a wife, children, and was a suburbanite. To bolster a sagging self-esteem he dominated five women plus his wife on a steady basis. He could not commit to a woman (his wife) nor did he want to leave her. He ran around, made money and wasted a good deal of it on the expenses of the women, and the masochistic acceptance of a dominating accountant he had hired. The accountant was a major "Gonife," a crook, a swindler and quite aggressive and threatening.

Ethan's wife was fearful of losing her husband, was quite attached to him and may have loved him. She allowed his behavior as long as he saw her Saturday and Saturday night. The children saw him as an absent, hard-working man who they could not understand. They (two of them) were resentful and sought out uncles and aunts for their needs.

Elias believed the business problem, the complaint of ET, had to wait. He had to uncover and intervene in the gross destructiveness ET and his wife were suffering. When Elias made this decision, he knew ET could quit; however, he counted on the healthful features in ET to grasp this importance. He also thought Mrs. T would go along because another outside force (his ego and super-ego) could add to her for the strength needed to observe and maybe change things.

By the way, I notice I use "he" for the character Elias and my own thinking when I plunge in to explain Elias— forgive me if you can, and if not OK.

So, with great authority Elias demanded to see all the parties, except the accountant, in this ménage of plenty. Elias had to *shake up* this folly.

It worked. ET was humiliated, his wife wrathful—she woke up. ET's early maternal needs for caring and support were directed to his wife, who responded with care and sensuality in the treatment. She became the strong one at that moment

And therapy really began. The accountant was taken care of by the Manhattan DA, the police—another story of ET finding himself. The five women went away (see the session). Mrs. T started treatment with another therapist—yet another story. Elias worked with ET and the family—yet another story

## SUSAN D.

A great struggle internally for Elias, which he battled consciously and unconsciously. Because of his own life issues and his then personal conflicts, this patient awoke his desires and yearnings. A great intrapsychic battle ensued which he was aware of. He knew his job; he knew Susan's unconscious battles, her ability to take her primitive infant yearnings, her strengths as she became a successful lawyer, to punish her parents without warmth and regard. She was dreadfully lonely and self-destructive—yet appealing. This case represents Elias's struggle for what he needed: maternal, sensual and sexual bonding, and a longing that could never be fulfilled

## CAPTAIN G.

The saddest outcome. Here the system, including Elias, failed the man. Much more intervention, much more seeking into the mind of Captain G needed to be done, as well as understanding the loss of his wife, the grind and wear he was undergoing. On top of PTSD lay the depressive longing of an aging professional. His supervisors, his colleagues at the precinct, the psychiatric police team, did not do a good enough job in putting the pieces together. Elias should have refused the case because it smelled of nitroglycerine. Elias had experienced it with the (Frank Todd case), where he and the referring agency did not understand the meaning of treatment in secret from the husband. She needed social work intervention, a team to help her leave and protect her. Then she needed an analytic intervention.

Elias saw people in need from 6am to 8pm. At times, he understood the need for anonymity or secrecy. Elias chose to take on the needs of CEOs, crime bosses and their families, long distance truckers who were only available at odd times. And as such, had a rich and rewarding practice. Moreover, he was heartbroken about his own family and he needs to find the strength and resilience to continue.

# ACKNOWLEDGMENTS

I wish to thank a number of people who helped me mobilize my thoughts and flesh out the characters of this novel. First of all, Arthur Friedman who thought that there were many interesting stories to tell about people's pathos. Second, to Mitchell Maxwell who sat through my ruminations and ideas and translated them into meaningful stories. I'd also like to thank Freenie Baker for the final edit of this work, along with Lou Aronica and The Story Plant.

Thanks to Dr. Marianne Gillow for collegial work for the past two decades and Mya Kagan for her input and suggestions as the work progressed. Ilene and Gadi Rosenfeld were influential in their thinking about this book, as well as my sons, Garvey and David.

I also of course wish to thank my wife, children, and grandchildren and my dog Sasha (a golden Hovawat) for their patience and support since they gave up time with me so I could concentrate on this work.

# ABOUT THE AUTHOR

**Dr. Manny Rich** has been practicing as a psychoanalytic and psychodynamic therapist for fifty-six years. He is currently teaching analytic theory for the Chinese American Alliance, as well as supervising advanced and beginning students in the science and art of analytic practice.

Dr. Rich received his Doctorate in Human Relations from NYU in 1972 and received a certification from Post Graduate Center of Mental Health in Psychoanalysis, Psychotherapy and Training and Supervision of the Psychoanalytic Process for new and experienced therapists. He also holds an MSW and Certification of Mental Health Consultation and Applied Principals of Psychoanalytic Process for corporations and public institutions to solve internal struggle and misaligned structure. Combined, he has 15 years of post-college education.

In his spare time, Dr. Rich plays the saxophone, is an avid target shooter and survivalist, spends time with his family, and works on his upstate New York property.

Dr. Rich comes from a classic early-1900's-immigrant-to-New-York-City-family migration from violent persecution in Eastern Europe. It is from this experience he became what is commonly known now as a survivalist. He grew up during World War II and worried that the same thing happening in Europe at the time could happen in New York: a breakdown in society, where the police and governing protection collapse and survival tactics are necessary to protect his family.

It is this history that paints his lifelong relationship with guns. In psychoanalytic terms, a gun represents the need for power, the fear of authority and the extension of the penis among many others. Dr. Rich grew up in Williamsburg, Brooklyn near the Brooklyn Navy Yard, where his father worked on Navy battleships during World War II and later owned a hardware store.

Growing up in New York City, Dr. Rich was the grandson of Jews who escaped violent persecution in Eastern Europe, not from the Germans, but Slavic anti-Jewish gangs who, with local government approval, would kill and plunder Jewish towns for their money and treasure just before World War I in 1915.

His father was hunted through the Romanian woods, losing family on the way to a boat that landed him in New York City. His mother's family of eight teenage boys was led by his grandfather, who was an ironsmith and made knives and swords as well as fire escapes and steel window shutters. The steel shutters saved the family from an attack on their village, giving them a moment to arm up and fight their way through marauding Cossacks to their last stop, Brooklyn, New York.

Imagine your parents' and grandparents' violent escape from European Jewish persecution and 30 years later the Nazis in Germany coming to power and American Nazis filling a rally at New York's Madison Square Garden just before the start of World War II.

In the Jewish neighborhoods of Brooklyn, Manny Rich's family was stocked with guns, ammunition and food, target shooting in their basements on their days off. This survivalist mentality combined with America's Second Amendment right to bear arms, drives Mr. Rich's belief that the right to bear arms in America ensured that no matter how corrupt or prejudiced the local police and government could become, no Nazi rally at the Garden would have had an easy time Jew-hunting in Brooklyn that night.

A childhood fascination with winning World War II, guns and survival tactics mixed with working at his father's hardware store in Williamsburg and a strong emphasis on education produced the first in the family's history of college graduates, as Dr. Rich earned his college degree from New York University.

Dr. Rich has been a card-carrying member of the NRA since the age of 18. At Boys High School of Brooklyn he was on the rifle team, in college at New York University, he was a member of Perishing Rifle Squad and the ROTC Rifle Team, and he was licensed by the NRA in 1960 to teach competitive marksmanship. He also played saxophone from the time he was in grammar school through his college marching band.

In his early teens, the FBI showed up at his parents' door after Dr. Rich innocently ordered a World War Two 59-inch anti-tank gun he was going to use as a tie rack. The FBI told his mother that they would arrest her if she accepted delivery, so Dr. Rich bought another tie rack.

His father worked at Brooklyn Navy Yards from 1939 to 1948 as an electrician. Notable in history, his father Leo Rich worked on the electric and lighting in the ceremonial area of the Missouri battleship for the anticipated surrender of the Japanese in World War II. The Japanese signed their surrender there on September 2, 1945.

Dr. Rich's fascination with guns includes a dedication to gun safety through education and training that includes impulse control. He believes that gun sports along with the right to bear arms comes with the responsibility of safety, discipline, training and dedication to ensure responsible and safe usage to minimize accidents that in reality are mental distortions played out in real time.

Suicides in America account for 55% of all gun deaths in America, and Dr. Rich believes suicides are also responsible for a sizable number of the unexamined 30,000 car deaths per year in America considered accidents.

Dr. Rich believes that once America gets past the negative stigma associated with mental health, we can address the needless gun violence and self-destructiveness by properly training all gun owners in America so we all can live safely and politically free, without any political litmus test on gun rights.

Dr. Rich blogs about issues of the day on his website MannyRich.com and invites you to comment or reach him there.